TILL DEATH DO US PART...

Bianca opened the door on total darkness. The room reeked of perfume. When she switched on the light she saw the broken bottle and the savage disorder of her room. Someone had been there, someone searching wildly and frantically for something.

But the room had only been searched. Nothing had been taken. Whoever her enemy was, he was not a burglar . . . but he could be her ex-husband . . . *and he could be a killer. . . .*

Katie

Season of Evil

Elsie Lee

A DELL BOOK

Published by
DELL PUBLISHING CO., INC.
1 Dag Hammarskjold Plaza
New York, N.Y. 10017

Dell ® TM 681510, Dell Publishing Co., Inc.

ISBN: 0-440-17599-2

Reprinted by arrangement with the author.

Printed in the United States of America

First Dell printing—September 1977

Chapter
1

"For heaven's sake, *put on your glasses*," Julian hissed as we came out of the courthouse. I had just enough consciousness left to shield my face from the photographers skipping up and down the steps, trying for angle shots—but of course the glasses were *in* the handbag.

They would be.

I have never been prepared for anything in my life. I have to buy nothing but plain black or white underwear; otherwise I wind up with only a peach-colored slip the day I meant to wear a sheer white blouse. If James Bond had ever met me, he'd be dead by now.

Let's face it: I am a bumbler, and not even my mother was particularly fond of me.

Ludo had used to say I was a genius of absurdity and more fun than people to have around, but I'd just been told very legally that, after four years of marriage, he preferred people after all.

The steps were shallow . . . the better for crawling up, I suppose, but between tears of despair, and holding that damned handbag in front of my face, I was jolted off balance. If Julian had only been holding my arm—but he didn't want the relationship emphasized because of his firm—and what with nothing to hold onto and unable to see, my heel caught. Next thing I knew, I was catapulting down the steps on top of a photographer.

We wound up on the sidewalk, breathless and sprawling. "I'm so sorry," I managed to say, while he was examining the camera tenderly. "I didn't mean to, I tripped . . ."

"It's okay," he said, and turned suddenly, avidly. By his expression I knew he thought it was worth any number of bruises to get an exclusive picture of the former Mrs. Ludovic DeCourcy Trael. All Julian's care, my hideous dark glasses and brimmed hats, all the flying phalanx of attorneys around me, were wasted—because I could never do anything right. I couldn't even get down a flight of shallow courthouse steps.

I looked up at the sharp ferrety face bending over me—he'd probably get a bonus for this—and I burst into tears. "*Please!* I'll let you take a proper picture, but not this—Ludo'd die of embarrassment. Please, no!"

His camera wavered slightly. "After what came out in court, why d'you care?" he demanded in surprise— and lost his chance, because I rolled over and up to my knees.

"It wasn't any of it true, don't you *know* that?" I babbled distractedly. "I don't know any more about what's going on than you do—and will you please for God's sake help me up? I've broken the heel of my shoe."

Julian and Mr. Abelson were hurrying down the steps towards me, while the photographer dragged me erect. "If it wasn't true, why'd you let him get away with it?"

"Did you ever try to argue with fifty million dollars?"

"That's enough," Abelson was saying authoritatively. "Don't say *anything*, Mrs. Trael."

"Hey!" the photographer protested, as Julian pushed him away and I was being rushed toward a taxi. "You promised me . . ."

"Not now," Julian said, tight-lipped.

"But I did promise . . ."

"Not now!"

The photographer dogged us determinedly, trying for his shot, frustrated by my brother and his lawyer. I had a glimpse of Ludo himself, running the gauntlet of newspapermen at the far end of the courthouse steps . . . so he had been in court all the time. "You'll miss Mr. Trael," I told my bird-dog bitterly. "He's just coming out, over there . . ."

"The hell with him. I want you and you *promised*," he snarled—and it was true, I had, but Julian shoved me into a cab.

"What's your name?"

"Jim Denton, *Sun-Courier*," he said automatically, as Julian climbed in beside me and slammed the door, while Abelson said "Get going!" to the driver and the cab started forward.

I leaned to the open window. "1022 St. Regis, tomorrow," I said rapidly. Fair's fair; I had agreed— and what difference did it make now, anyway? Julian pulled me back and closed the window roughly—but the sharp features flashed a cocky grin as Denton stepped back. He mouthed something I couldn't hear, and made the Churchill V-sign. It was obscurely comforting; nobody had been smiling at me for a long long while.

Julian wasn't smiling now, either. "Really, Bianca!"

"Would you have preferred a picture of your sister flat on her back at the foot of the courthouse steps?" I asked coldly. "What divine headline possibilities; 'Dr. Julian Robinson's sister, tossed from the courthouse by Mr. Ludovic Trael, lies sobbing on the pavement of Foley Square . . .'"

"No, no, of course not," Julian said hurriedly. "Bianca, please control yourself."

"Why?"

"There's something behind this," Abelson frowned.

"I'm not up to Anscot, Vermuhlen and Talbott, I told you that to begin with—but we had a perfectly pleasant conference. At least, I thought it was agreed Mrs. Trael wouldn't contest, asked nothing, and we'd handle the case with dignity—and then, in court, they produce this sensationalism. I do not understand it."

"That makes two of us," I said dully. "It was all a big lie; I never knew that man in the pictures; I never spent a night with him anywhere, whatever they say. I've never even met a man named George in my whole life . . ."

"Oh, nonsense, Bi," Julian objected literally. "*Everybody* meets someone named George at least once."

"Where did they get those pictures?" Abelson went on. "You recognized the dress; the maid identified the negligee, and unfortunately," he coughed delicately "the court was forced to accept your husband's recognition of—the other pictures."

"I don't know. I don't know who did what nor why, Mr. Abelson, I only know it wasn't I."

"They couldn't put a date to anything; all they had were the pictures. Did you ever get involved with some of your 'interesting characters'," Julian's voice was a faint sneer, "about whom you knew nothing— who might have drugged or hypnotized you?"

"No," I said flatly, "and just because, *once*, I met a student at the Sorbonne who probably told some disreputable friends to steal mother's pearls," I added angrily, "doesn't mean I usually consort with criminals or pimps, dammit. You know Jean-Daniel was never in my apartment; it was conjecture. The Sureté did their best, but even the inspector never blamed me."

"Yes, well, they did prove you'd brought home a perfect stranger when Ludo was out of the country," Julian retorted. "Someone you'd picked up in a bar . . ."

"The Oyster Bar in Grand Central," I snarled, "and he was a teen-ager who'd got separated from his 4-H

Club group on the way to the Fair. He couldn't remember the hotel where they were staying; naturally, I brought him home to phone his folks for directions —and his mother cried all over me with relief that I'd taken care of him. He was about fourteen!"

"But in court," Abelson murmured thoughtfully, "the servants testify only to a stranger, aren't asked his age, but encouraged to create an impression he was a male pickup, with a strong implication that he was only one of a string. Why didn't you tell me this before?"

"I was too totally stunned—and if you recall, the law didn't permit me to say a word in my own defense."

"Yes. We stipulated no contention; we couldn't reverse—and that is precisely what I don't understand," Abelson remarked. "With everything cut and dried, why did AVT produce these fireworks?"

"That's where I came in," I said wearily, but he was still cogitating when we drew up before the hotel.

"Go directly to the suite, Bianca," Julian ordered, leaning forward to pay the driver. "Don't look at anyone, don't stop for anything, you understand?"

"Maybe you'd like me to ring one of those little bells they used in Ben Hur?" I asked. "For the lepers. And maybe I should cry 'unclean, unclean' at the same time?"

He had the grace to flush. "I'm only thinking of you," he said stiffly, and I felt slightly ashamed of my temper—because it was kind of him to leave his job and fly up from Maracaibo to stand behind me these past weeks. Particularly, as I knew now, when he didn't believe a word I said.

"Oh, the hell with it," I muttered and crawled out of the cab lopsided, due to the missing heel of my shoe. To my surprise, Abelson briskly accompanied us.

"I'll come up for a minute," he stated, bracing my elbow with amazing firmness, so that we were somehow up the entrance steps, through the revolving door and across the lobby in a kind of skimming trot ending in a vacant elevator—while Julian was ascending the *other* entrance steps and fending off the concerted rush of reporters with distaste. "Eleven," said the lawyer calmly, silencing my involuntary correction with a hideous grimace. We walked into the carpeted eleventh floor hall; the metal grille clashed shut; the elevator plummeted downward.

"What is this in aid of?" I asked, blankly.

"There are indicators on elevators," he said. "Some sharp fellow has watched where the elevator let us off; when Julian comes up to the tenth floor, there will be major uncertainty among the beagles below." He chuckled placidly, and suggested, "Take off your shoes, the better to walk quickly down one flight— before some enterprising chap finds a service lift."

"I had no idea how much cloak-and-dagger is required of lawyers," I told him breathlessly, when we'd gained the safety of the suite.

"Oh yes, we learn a number of clever little dodges. There's more to Perry Mason than meets the eye," he remarked with a smile. "Go along to the living room, Mrs. Trael, until Julian gets here."

There was still some ice in the insulated bucket. "What d'you like?" I called. He expressed a preference for bourbon and soda, if we had it—and we did, because that's Julian's tipple. I had just got the highballs ready when my brother nipped into the suite, looking hot and flustered. "Calm down over this," I extended the glass.

"My God, for the first time in my life I *need* a drink," he grunted. "I never dreamed, never had the least idea, it'd be like this."

"Or you wouldn't have come?"

"Perhaps not!" he snapped. "Dammit, Bi—I've wasted several weeks and thousands of dollars only to find there wasn't a damn thing I or anyone else could do for you." He took a long gulp of the high-ball, fumbling for a cigarette with nervous fingers. "Sid would have taken the case on phoned instructions from me, but no! I have to come up here to provide backing for our family. Backing, hah!" he snorted. "I don't know what in hell you've been up to, but apparently they've got you dead to rights, kiddie!"

"Well, as to that, I'm not so sure," Sidney Abelson said. "That's why I'm here. Sit down, Julian, for heaven's sake, and let me talk to your sister."

"What's to say?" Julian muttered, but he sat down and relapsed into silence.

"For one thing," the lawyer said slowly, "I may be an egotistical idiot, but I pride myself on smelling truth—and I think Mrs. Trael is telling the truth. That is," he added carefully, "*the truth as she sees it.* She may be wrong; if so, it is an honest error." He took a sip of his drink, set it aside, and placed his neatly manicured fingers tip to tip—the apotheosis of middle-aged family attorney, but I wasn't laughing at him.

"My reasoning is this," he said neatly. "*Why* the unnecessary filth? What did they think she could do to throw the case out of court? Why was it essential to discredit her publicly, because that's what it amounts to.

"Who, now, will believe a word Bianca Robinson Trael may say?" he shrugged. "So the question arises, my dear Bianca," he smiled placidly, "I may call you Bianca, may I not, after knowing Julian for so many years? I expect you won't like constantly being called 'Mrs. Trael'?"

"Of course—except it's still my name, isn't it?"

"According to Emily Post, you are Mrs. Robinson Trael. No matter." He narrowed his eyes once more and stared into space. "What could you have said?" he mused.

"Nothing, obviously," Julian said impatiently. "She

was completely tongue-tied during the whole thing. What are you getting at, Sid?"

"That if we can establish any hanky-panky, throw even the least shadow of a doubt on the authenticity of those photographs, we can throw the case out of court, reverse the divorce decree, institute suit for defamation of character, prevent a possible second marriage for Ludovic Trael (if that's what he was working on), and quite legally tie him in knots."

There was a long silence, while Sid replenished his highball and mine. "But I don't want to tie Ludo in knots," I said honestly.

"What do you want, Bi?"

"I want to know *why*. Listen—it all happened practically within five minutes. One morning, I was a happy woman, married to a man who loved me. We're all adults," I said baldly. "Ludo and I were happy to the point we'd—loved each other twice the previous night. We had breakfast, we kissed each other goodbye for the day—and when I got home at four o'clock that afternoon," I gulped at the memory, *"his lawyer tells me Mr. Trael has instituted suit for divorce.*

"The only time I ever saw him again was in the presence of three lawyers, a stenographer and a tape recorder. He threw the pictures across the desk at me, and . . . Oh, please," I sniffled, "I told you everything at the start."

Of course, the real last time I'd seen Ludo was this very day—when he must have been sitting in court, listening to his lawyers urbanely making hash of my reputation, while I was too caught off balance to think of a word in defense. I hadn't known he was there until, struggling to my feet on the sidewalk, I'd glimpsed the broad-shouldered figure, the crisp-curled russet hair above Viking blue eyes averted from me—retreating implacably, indifferently, from the idiotic stupid woman he'd married and discarded.

"Yes," Sid was saying, "I know you told me, but I still say it's only truth as you see it—and perhaps you aren't seeing all the truth. No," he held up a hand, "let me finish. Mr. Trael left—when?"

"Oh, I don't know—nine-thirty or ten, perhaps."

"You went out—when?"

"About noon. I did a little shopping, met a friend for lunch at Armando's. Grace Peters, you remember her?" I turned to Julian, who nodded morosely. "We hadn't met since college, so it was a long lunch. When we parted, I walked home; I window shopped, took my time, so it was nearly four before I got back."

"What difference does it make?" Julian was impatient.

"Only that whatever happened occurred within six hours that particular day," Sid pointed out. "We can even say it must have been less; there had to be time for Mr. Trael to consult his lawyers, make initial arrangements, to a point that by four o'clock it was a *fait accompli*. There was an immense amount to do, you know, and even for its most important client, AVT couldn't move any faster than its secretaries could type. There had to be private, summit-type, phone calls to influential people in order to get the suit on the docket within a week. New York divorce courts are always at least three, sometimes six months behind. So. He'd reach his office—when?"

"Fifteen minutes by cab; half an hour if he walked, and he always did unless he was late for an appointment or it was a really stormy day."

"But that was a pleasant day, because after lunch, you strolled home," Abelson reflected, "so we can't rule out the possibility he met someone on the street. You see what I'm getting at?" Julian was listening alertly now, nodding his head, but I drew a complete blank. Sid smiled at me. "Your husband had either a phone call, a letter, or a visitor during that morning who put a flea in his ear that laid the powder train," he explained. "If we could lay hands on his appointment book, and office phone and mail records for that day, it might tell us who your enemy is, Bianca."

"Enemy?"

"Someone has gone to a great deal of trouble to fake those pictures, my dear," he said quietly. "Someone who wished to convince your husband you were unfaithful to him, to cause him to repudiate you, disgrace you publicly, and remove you forever from his life. Now who would that person be? Think!"

I stared at my toes, hating myself for trembling. I don't have to think," I said finally. "It was—Ludo himself."

"But you just said . . ." Julian began. Sid held up a quelling hand.

"Why do you say that?"

"You said I only told the truth as I saw it," I said shakily. "Maybe this is it: I only thought he loved me, because he could kiss me and—make love to me. But now I remember . . .

"There was something on his mind for several months. He was—oh, abstracted sometimes, and in and out of town. Not really away; just a night or two —and that was unusual because it was always unexpected. I mean, he'd go off in the morning, and late in the afternoon, David—David Corey, his executive assistant—would phone to say Ludo was detained, not to expect him for dinner, or that he wouldn't be home tonight."

"Did you never comment, never ask about this?"

I shook my head, concentrating on memory. "There were phone calls. Ludo has an unlisted phone in his dressing room. Several times when I came in unexpectedly, he hung up abruptly—and once I was looking for Victor, the phone was ringing and I picked it up automatically. It went dead as soon as I said hello. At the time, I assumed it had been ringing for some time and the caller had got tired—I wonder."

"If a woman answers, hang up?" Abelson murmured. "Hmmm. Would you expect another woman, Bianca?"

"In a way. He had a *shocking* reputation; he never made any secret of it. That was why he insisted on marrying me after only ten days: because if we were seen together more than three times, everyone would assume I was his newest mistress." I smiled mirthlessly. "Since I wasn't, he wouldn't have anyone think so; we'd marry first and court later. If it didn't work, he'd give me a divorce whenever I wanted—but I never did, of course, because I loved him all the time."

Abelson looked away tactfully, searching in various pockets. "You don't mind a pipe? I think better . . ."

"Of course." I was under control by the time he'd filled and lit up.

"May I be very blunt?" he asked finally. "As you said, we're adults. I'd like to probe—it might help."

"By all means."

"Were you a virgin when you married Ludovic Trael?" he inquired calmly.

"Yes," I said steadily, "and he knew it."

"Tell me about the courtship after marriage, please."

"Well—I moved into the Paris house, and sometimes he was there and sometimes he wasn't." I said helplessly. "You know he is a mining engineer, a special consultant for governments all over the world —and he has that huge freighter-turned-yacht so he can go anywhere."

"Yes. Go on."

"I was finishing research and writing my doctoral thesis; he'd stay a couple of weeks, taking me around town." I steeled myself against those memories: silly presents, extravagant flowers every day, long absurd phone conversations—from Ludo's private phone to mine, at the other end of the hall. "He was so proud when I got the Ph.D. in history. I'd have got it on my own, but the *summa cum laude* was Ludo, because he'd been everywhere and had legends I'd never have found by myself."

"Good heavens, are you *that* Robinson?" Abelson was genuinely startled. "*First Clues to History?*"

I nodded. "Ludo *would* send it to a publisher."

"I see. Well. When did the courtship end, when did you decide it was for real?"

"It was always for real, but Ludo insisted nothing should change—because it was so sudden, you know. We met at a faculty tea at the Sorbonne, and he said . . ." I reached for a cigarette in a futile effort to steady my voice. "He said he fell in love with me at first sight, but couldn't expect equal promptness on my part, so I must have time. I expect he had commitments, too. He hadn't planned on me, any more than I'd planned on him."

"You never told me this, Bi," Julian was half-angry.

"Why should I? My marital arrangements were no one's concern but mine," I pointed out, "but no matter how sudden, you scarcely *object* to Ludovic Trael for a brother-in-law."

He ran a harassed hand over his sparse hair. "I didn't; I thought he was a bit—old," he muttered, "but on the other hand, he'd look after you. Don't look so insulted, Bi," he said flatly. "Dammit, a good deal of the time you need a keeper. Trael's a rich man, fine family—he wouldn't be the first brilliant mind to fall for a beautiful dimwit."

"Robinson's *First Clues to History* is far from dim," Sid observed tactfully, but Julian was still temperish.

"Exactly. Bi's occupied with what's past and out of this world," he snapped. "Thank God she isn't an archaeologist, or she'd fall into every hole she dug! Marries a man she's known less than two weeks! I don't care if Trael is famous, now see what's happened!"

"I still think this a hole she didn't dig," Abelson returned. "Be quiet, Julian. I want the rest of this. When did the courtship end?"

"When we came back to New York. After that, I was expanding the thesis for a complete book. I only worked when Ludo was away, so it was months before I finished. Sometimes I went on the boat with him, whatever he wanted . . . He took me to the Caribbean for a couple of weeks, when I'd had a bad cold, and to Mexico for firsthand book material." I shrugged helplessly. "I can't think of anything else. You'd better ask questions."

"I shall," he said briskly. "Did your husband tell you when and where he was going?"

"When, but not where. He said if I didn't know, I couldn't inadvertently give anything away," I ignored Julian's snort, "and sometimes it was hush-hush for our government. There was radiophone on the boat and he spoke to the office every day; if I had a message, I phoned them to relay it, and they always let me know when to expect him."

"Did he never tell you anything about his work?"

"Yes, occasionally when he came back, but usually only generalities. Of course I could guess where he'd been by what he brought me, he always brought me something," I explained to Sid's raised eyebrows. "Not definitive, but if it were, oh—twenty pounds of macadamia nuts, he'd been to Hawaii or Australia—and silk is mostly Tokyo or Hong Kong, except velvet, which is France. You know . . ."

"No, but evidently you do, Bianca." He laughed heartily. "Did Trael ever realize your knowledge of exports, I wonder?"

"I don't know. I never thought about it until now."

"We're out of ice," Julian announced. "I'll get more, and I'd better check plane reservations. Sid, answer the door?"

Abelson nodded absently, and Julian went away to

the bedroom phone. "I take it you were perfectly
faithful to Mr. Trael during his absences," he remarked suddenly, "but what about him?" He smiled
at my blank expression. "I've heard his reputation,
too," he murmured, "and a private boat is—very con-
venient. Bluntly, do you think he was alone?"

"I don't *know*, but yes—I did think so."

"Why so trusting?"

"For the same reason you said you believed me,"
I told him slowly, "and because—he was always so
glad to get back to me." I could feel myself flushing
furiously, but Sid's eyes were merely impersonally
appraising.

"That figures. You must have made a breathtaking
couple: Mr. Trael has exactly the coloring and buc-
caneering physique to complement your black hair
and white skin. Sir Francis Drake or Leif Ericson,
paired with Undine."

"He thought—Melisande," I said in a small voice,
as there was a knock on the door.

"Room service—but cuddle on the couch, in
case . . ."

I crouched sideways, pulling up my feet. *Would I
ever be able to face the world again?* Reason said I'd
be no news in a few more hours. Thanks to Julian and
Abelson, nobody'd ever got a picture of me, except
the photograph of Dortret's portrait, which some enterprising reporter must have bribed out of Customs,
because Ludo'd only kept the thing in order to laugh
at it. No one would ever recognize Mrs. Robinson
Trael from *that* painting.

Ice bucket in hand, Sidney Abelson looked down
at me reflectively. "I don't believe in another woman,"
he said quietly. "I think Ludovic Trael was wholly,
completely, insanely in love with you—to the point
that those pictures maddened him with disillusion.
Had he a violent temper?" I nodded. "There you are,

then." He set the ice on the tray while I sat up abruptly, smoothing my skirt.

"You're so right," I agreed cynically. "That's *me*— right there behind the eight-ball. Well, I've plenty of temper myself, as well as disillusion. If Ludo'd loved me and there's no other woman, why refuse me any chance to talk to him?

"After four years, he can take one look at some dirty photographs and instantly believe them?" I cried passionately. "He might be terribly shocked, but if he'd *loved* me—when I denied them, he'd have gone hell for leather to prove me right or wrong." I sprang up, pacing back and forth nervously. "*Why didn't he?*"

"Because he knew where they came from, he'd had them made in order to get rid of me—and that's the worst," I choked. "All he ever had to do was say, 'Binks, it didn't work out for me after all—divorce, please.' I'd have agreed, no matter how I cried in private. That was our bargain. What did I do that made him not trust me to keep it?"

I flung around to face Sid, standing glass in hand, watching me intently. "I wasn't extravagant; I never spent half the allowance he gave me. *He* bought the furs and jewels, not I; I only wore them to please him. I'm not a mink and diamond sort of woman. So *why* the care to prevent financial demands from me?"

"What did he say when you finally did see him?"

"Nothing. He only agreed because I flatly said I wouldn't leave without. I suppose he was growing tired of living on the boat," I said bitterly, "and they couldn't throw me out bodily. He wouldn't even see me in decent privacy . . . I *told* you all this . . .

"He threw the pictures across the desk at me, and said 'What more explanation do you need?' " I closed my eyes in remembered nausea. "That's the only time I ever saw the things. I wasn't let to touch them; I suppose they thought I'd tear them up and *eat* them or something. I knew the dress was mine, it had a distinctive neckline, but *I never saw that man in my life.*"

"What did you say?"

"*The* wrong thing, of course," I smiled grimly. "I told you I have a temper, too. So while someone was carefully scooping up the pictures, I—well, I couldn't believe it, you know. I said to Ludo, 'Those aren't me —you've been had. How much did they ask you? Don't pay a cent!'

"And he stood up and said, 'I shan't—you're damn right I've been had—and I hope George can support you in the style to which you're accustomed.' And when I got back upstairs, the safe was hanging open with all the jewelry gone, and all the furs removed from the closet. You know. You had to raise hell to get back the old beaver coat I'd bought for myself, or I wouldn't even have had a winter coat. I'm surprised they didn't take all my dresses."

"Against the law," Abelson remarked absently. "Husband is required to provide food, shelter and clothing commensurate with his financial position. Strictly speaking, for Trael's position, you were entitled to retain the furs and jewels."

"I didn't want them."

"I know. That's a point I made clear to Anscot."

"But *why* did he think I was a gold-digger?"

"I fancy that's part of whatever made him explode." He looked at his watch. "Lord, is it that time? I have to go." He polished off his drink, thumped the glass on the tray. "I confess I don't get it, but now I'm certain something exists to be gotten. I'm more sorry than I can say about the court session." He sighed sadly. "My first reaction was 'the smooth-talking bastards diddled me!' I was prepared to go to the Bar Association; I may still, although it might be our ace in the hole.

"It's ethical for lawyers to agree on procedure for

civil cases, in prior conference. Saves time for the judge when details are worked out beforehand—but it isn't ethical for a lawyer to abrogate that agreement when he gets into court, understand?

"And to all intents and purposes, that's what Anscot, Vermuhlen and Talbott did today," he said grimly, "and I shan't forget it. In the legal profession, AVT is Caesar's wife; I suspect it's only Trael's importance as a client that made them agree to represent him in a divorce action.

"What's more," Sid narrowed his eyes, "I could swear Anscot was as appalled as I. He was there, backing his junior, but I'm positive he hadn't the least idea . . . He'll have had the whole story of who gave what instructions by now, of course; I'll wager he's fit to be tied! He won't like the mere possibility of a Bar Association query, he won't like it *at all*. Yes, I think that's our entering wedge, Bianca."

"What do you mean?"

Abelson shrugged thoughtfully. "Anscot respects me, even if I'm small potatoes beside AVT. He won't like a possible complaint from me," Sid said with dignity. "He'll be receptive to full disclosure, in private—over lunch at India House."

"What could he tell you that would help?"

"Who altered the instructions to his junior," he said promptly, "and he'll be disturbed by my reflections. He won't like to think AVT could be a party to false evidence, however innocently. He'll make every effort to get facts. I can tell you, Anscot'll be better than a bloodhound if I can unsettle him sufficiently! That firm is his wife, mistress, children, his life; he'll do anything short of murder to maintain its purity— and I don't know," he finished thoughtfully, "why I except murder."

"We want your husband's appointments, phone calls, letters received and dictated for the 4th of April," said Sid. "Anscot will get them for us, no matter who he has to bribe!" He chuckled wickedly, and somehow I was laughing with him.

"What's so funny?" Julian asked stiffly, coming back from the phone.

"Sid's going to Delilah Mr. Anscot, to get us Ludo's appointment book . . ." I couldn't go any farther. Ludo'd said I was a genius of absurdity? Was there anything more totally mad than pitting my lawyer against his: two middle-aged, stuffily correct, unimpeachable members of the Bar Association, fencing slyly over Nasi Goreng in the un-incensed air and clear purity of India House? *Good God!* I leaned on the back of the couch and very nearly had hysterics, until Sid got the picture and whinnied gently, while Julian stared at us blankly.

We sobered down after a moment. "I must go, Bianca," he held my hand firmly. "I don't know what I can do, but I shall try. Where will I reach you?"

"That's a good question," I said slowly, "and now you pose it, I wish I had an answer." It was quite true; I'd never thought about "where next?"

Well, I said it before: I am never prepared for anything until it is gibbering in the middle of the road before me.

With Julian and Sid looking startled, I made an effort. "I guess I still have some money; he couldn't close my account, could he? And I'd just had my quarterly allowance . . ."

"Savings account? Deposit box?" Sid asked alertly. "Where is your checkbook, incidentally?"

"In my handbag. I never had a savings account."

"Deposit box?" Julian inquired wearily. "I never thought to ask; sorry, Sid. Bi would forget her head if it weren't tied on—and sometimes I wonder if the thread isn't too loose."

"Do you mind letting me up from here?" I asked. "We've already established I'm a cretin, no? But do admit I have had other things on my mind than deposit boxes these past weeks."

"Of course. Was it a joint box?" Sid asked smoothly. "What was in it?"

"It was mine, but I think Ludo could open it."

"It'll be empty by now," Julian snorted.

"Not necessarily. What was in it?" Sid repeated.

That was another good question; what in hell had I put in the thing? "My will . . . the citations for Phi Bete and my doctorate . . . the Peale miniature of Sarah Pinckney Robinson. My birthday stocks," I remembered suddenly. "Ludo gave me a hundred shares of something every birthday."

"Oh, my God!" Julian groaned violently. "A hundred shares of *something*—she doesn't know what —and a Peale miniature and some diplomas. They're probably gone by now!"

Sid shook his head. "Pointless. Once registered in Bianca's name, the stocks were noncombackibus. I don't doubt the box was thoroughly examined, but its contents will still be there. However," he turned to the desk, "we must have a holograph will at once." He drew out a sheet of notepaper, extended his pen to me. "Write 'I, Bianca Robinson Trael, do hereby leave everything of which I die possessed to . . .' Put in any name you like; make it your usual handwriting, sign your full name, plus the date."

I inserted Julian's name, naturally, and Abelson twitched it away from me, swiftly appended his own name as a witness, folding the paper and sticking it in his pocket. "Have a proper will drawn as soon as possible," he instructed me. "This will cover things, meanwhile."

"I'm not likely to die," I protested. "I'm only twenty-nine and offensively healthy," but he merely patted my hand and turned to the door.

"Accidents happen," he said. "Now, where will you be?"

"I don't know. I—hadn't thought."

There was a long pause. "Chevy Chase," Julian sighed, reluctantly accepting the inevitable. His fingers slipped keys from his ring, extended them.

"House: one key for all doors, and toolshed . . . garage . . . car, trunk key in the glove compartment." He disinterred a card from his wallet. "Registration. Sid, call the insurance for me, will you? Arrange coverage for Bi, and pay if there's extra premium?"

"What about phone and utilities?"

"Never disconnected; the tenants pay or we deduct from security. The last people moved a week or two back; I'll have time to phone the agents not to re-rent." Julian ran a hand over his forehead vaguely. "Sorry to be unceremonious, Bi, but it's either six tonight or wait two days—and I should get back."

"Of course." Already nearly three? "You'll have to whiz! I'd better help you pack. Goodbye, Sid, and thanks for whatever!"

"Let me know if you leave Chevy Chase for even a night!" he said, authoritatively. "And *think*. If you remember even the slightest, silliest, apparently meaningless detail, call me at once! When will you check out here?"

"Better stay tonight, get the shuttle tomorrow, so you can market by daylight," Julian said. It sounded sensible; I nodded agreement. Sid brushed a fleeting kiss to my cheek, shook hands heartily with Julian, and departed.

Closing the door, my brother rubbed his hands together. "I'm starved! How about a sandwich? Order something, Bi . . ." I got roast beef sandwiches, side orders of cole slaw, and coffee. While Julian signed the slip and directed the waiter into the living room, I retrieved his bedroom slippers and found six handkerchiefs pushed to the rear of a drawer . . . "Soup's on," he called . . . while I dug out three packs of cigarettes in the bedside table, and picked up a monogrammed cuff link on the closet floor—leading to an immediate search for its mate, which turned up in his stud box, staring at me smugly . . .

"Where are you?" he inquired indistinctly. "I'm started, rude or not . . ." It was only another hour; Julian's spirits were rising in direct proportion.

I went out and eyed the food with loathing. *Have to eat, have to keep up your strength in time of travail* . . . Whoever said that? Someone who wasn't in travail, probably. I took a bite, laid the sandwich on the plate. "You're not eating," said Julian, demolishing his sandwich with strong white teeth that suddenly reminded me of a camel. "Got to keep up your strength, you know!"

"Stay me with flagons and comfort me with apples," I quoted irrepressibly. He did not pretend to misunderstand.

"All right, so you're sick of love," he said between gulps. "You'll get over it. You're young; you'll marry again." He eyed the uneaten sandwich on my plate. "If you're really not going to finish, I could use the other half?"

"Be my guest. You paid for it, after all." I drank some coffee and smoked in silence until he'd finished both sandwiches and cole slaw, sat back with a sigh of repletion, mopping his mouth in a series of dabs. He fumbled for a cigarette . . . and since he *is* my brother, even if seventeen years older than I, I knew something was bothersome. "*What?*" I asked baldly. He shifted uncomfortably in his chair, disconcerted by my sibling knowledge.

"Nothing," he mumbled, "except . . . well, remember Polly and I have to come back to that house next Fall."

"You'd rather I weren't chummy with neighbors? Be easy: the last thing I want is company," I said evenly.

"What *will* you do, Bi?" his voice was unexpectedly troubled.

"Lick my wounds for a while," I shrugged. "Then —I don't know. I could teach history . . . research for an archaeologist . . . I might even write. Historical novels sell fairly well." I smiled at him with genuine affection. Julian was my brother, after all, and it couldn't have been easy to find himself responsible for a teen-ager when he was only thirty, with a wife and babies.

"Don't worry, Juny," I said gently. "I've enough cash, and even if Ludo's blocked the account and cleared the box, there's always my ring." I held out my left hand, tipping it this way and that, sending a shower of brilliant green sparks about the darkening room. "I expect Ludo was *wild* at not being able to get this back," I said cynically, "but a woman's engagement and wedding rings are always her legal property, even after divorce."

I glanced fleetingly at the inch-square flawless emerald. "I know Polly thought it a bit vulgarly sized," I said with detachment, "but it may be my capital. Ludo insured it for fifty thousand; I expect I could pop it for half, no?"

"Pawn shops for *my* sister?" Julian was revolted. I always forget he has no lightness of touch . . .

"No, of course not, Juny!" I said quickly. "I only meant I've a portable asset in case of absolute disaster. Of *course* I wouldn't sell it; it's meant for Phebe's dowry. How is she, by the way?"

"Had a raise, and thinking of taking a leave of absence for a doctorate," he said absently, scribbling at the desk. "Here," he dropped a scrap of paper into my lap: a check for a thousand dollars. "You'd better have something, in case. If there's any financial problem, go to Lennart at Riggs Bank; he'll see you through until you can cable me, understand?" He eyed the

ring. "My God, I never knew it was worth so much.
Chevy Chase is safe enough—but it's a detached
house, you'll be alone . . . and why you'd want to be
reminded . . ." he muttered. "To please me, give it to
Lennart to hold?"

"Of course, if you think best," but he was still uneasy. I stood up briskly. "Get going, sweetie, or you'll
miss the plane."

He looked at his watch automatically and blenched.
"Christ! Where'n hell are the tickets—where's the bellboy—did I forget anything?"

"No, I checked. I'm very good for that," I assured
him, as there was a knock at the door. "There's the
boy *cum* tickets." Julian handed over luggage, told the
boy, "I'll meet you downstairs at the desk, have a
taxi ready for Kennedy Airport." He turned back to
me: a medium sort of man, undecided about anything not directly concerned with his career—with
eye-colored eyes and incipient myopia . . . a tan top-
coat slung over his arm and an expression of mingled
relief ("I did my duty; it's nearly over") and uneasi-
ness ("She's my sister; will she be all right?")

"I shall be perfectly all right," I assured him
brightly. "I shall have dinner here—I may even go to
a movie."

"I wouldn't, Bi," he said hastily. "Be sure to wear
the glasses; there'll still be reporters, I'm afraid. I'll
settle the bill, that holds everything until two tomorrow." He was still troubled. "I wish I could have
taken you down, seen you safe, but you understand?
It's tonight—or two days?"

"Will you *please* stop worrying? You sound like
something in the Third Man! It was only a phony divorce!"

Julian was unexpectedly serious. "Yes, that's what
it looks like." He flushed awkwardly. "I didn't believe
you, Bi—you knew it—but after Sid talked this after-

noon . . . I know him. He isn't kidding when he says
you have an enemy." His face twisted slightly. "Bi,
I couldn't bear if anything happened to you."

It was more emotion than I'd ever seen from Julian.
Impulsively, I ran forward to hug him. "*Nothing* will
happen," I assured him. "It's only—psychological
readjustment needed. I'll hide out in your house,
think it through. Don't worry, us Robinson's always
come out okay in the end!"

He smiled at my dramatic voice. "You're to let me
know *at once* if anything breaks?"

"Scout's honor, or whatever it is," I nodded. "Thanks
a million for the lend of the house; give my love to
Polly, have a smooth trip." I hugged him again convulsively. "Thank you more than I can ever say for
coming," I whispered.

"Nonsense!" he said, crossly. "But next time, could
you please try to think a bit first? None of this would
have happened . . . Oh, well," he sighed ruefully, "I
have to go or I'll miss the plane—and you've had
enough ears pinned back for one year." He threw an
arm around me, cuddled me against him for a moment, kissed my cheek firmly. "Brat!" said Julian,
pulling open the door. "I love you—but *don't* do it
again?"

Chapter
2

I went back to the living room and shook the coffee thermos experimentally: still a cupful, lukewarm but drinkable. I lit a cigarette and sipped.

Well. Here we are. Alone at last.

It was suddenly an alarming thought. I hadn't been alone for over four years; perhaps I'd forgotten how? Even when Ludo was away, there were servants, and for the first year, Rafe Trael and his wife, Helen, had lived with us.

I'd never lived in New York, though it's an easy city to learn, but Helen knocked herself out for me. Introductions, parties, shopping tips—because we were friends at first glance. She was willowy, tall, assisted-blonde, but it fitted her green eyes and faintly florid skin. "Presumably only my hairdresser knows for sure," she admitted with a grin, "but otherwise—ugh, Mouse Brown!"

Helen was eight years older than I, enormously Social, sophisticated and chic. Within a week we'd established a *petit dejeuner* in my bedroom after the men had gone. It was Helen who told me all the family gossip Ludo'd never mentioned. "My dear," she sighed dramatically, "*men* never think you could be *interested* in old Aunt Clara who plucked chickens for fun—or the reason for the barred top-story windows was Uncle Max."

"*Was* there a Max or Clara?"

"Among the *Traels?*" she scoffed incredulously.

"Don't be absurb; they'd drown a black sheep at birth!"

Rafe was the middle brother; the baby was Perryn, ten years younger than Ludo. There'd been a sister who died in infancy. Rafe managed the family businesses for Ludo. "Perryn's a playboy," Helen reported. "He's meant to be managing a ranch in New Mexico, but he finds plenty of time to ski at Chamonix or feed the kitty at Monte Carlo."

There was a family trust fund, dating from clipper-ship days, administered by the family, which at present was Ludo. It went automatically from father to son, but there were various ramifications, and apparently the thing could be dissolved by now. I gathered Rafe rather wished for his share outright, but as all three shared equally and there was plenty, Helen said, "What does it matter? Except Rafe could probably increase his own capital; he's a whiz in the market . . . and Ludo's thinking about dissolving.

"Old Ludo could have, too, but he wouldn't. *Heavens,* you're lucky never to have come up against him, Binks! The most frightening old autocrat with Emperor Franz Josef mustaches," she shuddered. "We all had to live here, you know—breakfast at eight, and everyone had to be there! God, the mornings I had to get up at six in order to put Rafe under a cold shower . . .

"*I* was permitted one morning a month," Helen simpered shyly, while I was convulsed with laughter. "All the same, it wasn't funny," she said soberly. "Two *years,* Binks!"

"And then you got stuck to manage the house for Ludo," I sympathized. "Oh, poor *you!*"

"Well, as to that," she grinned, "the *day* after the funeral, *I* established breakfast on trays when rung for! Ludo didn't care, and he was away so often. Heavens, it was *fun,*" Helen giggled. "I used the best china every day, and we drank the best wine ourselves. Old Ludo must have been *twirling!*"

I laughed heartily, but privately I loved Helen next

to Ludo. After ten years of hostessing the entire house, I thought most women would have resented me. She admitted it was *hell* adjusting to the top floor. "I'm forever forgetting we can't have more than two for dinner, or six for buffet," she remarked lightly—but neither then nor later did Helen ever say a word or look a look that was less than loving kindness. We were instantly friends, later we were intimate friends, until at last we were truly sisters. I'm not sure the men ever realized how close and companionable we were, as women, although I know Ludo was relieved.

He was a bit *stiff* to find they hadn't moved before we returned from Paris, but of course it was sensible to put a kitchen on the top floor and stay until they found the right buy. Heaven knows, we didn't need the top floor at that point. It was good luck for me, too. At the end of the first month I said to Helen, "May I *cast* myself on your mercy, pet?"

"Of course," she said, surprised, looking at me owlishly over her copy of the *Times*. "What can I do?"

"Take back the management of the house till I finish my book?" I said promptly. "I am going *out* of my mind. I am no sooner mentally lost in Brattahlid and Eystribyggd than Esther reports crisis in the kitchen, requiring immediate decision or total impasse—with forty guests for dinner; Or: the flowers have come; they didn't have bronze chrysanthemums and have sent pink gladioli with blue daisies instead—necessitating a different cloth and china service.

"I haven't time to keep the party book up to date—to the point I repeated a menu out of desperation, and wouldn't you know four of the guests were here both nights?" I waited tragically, while Helen chuckled. "And now Ludo's making noises about taking me to Mexico in the indeterminate but very near future—so *would* you, *could* you, cope for me? The alternative is hire someone—and I think we'd hate her, don't you?"

"Don't be silly," said Helen. "Of course I don't mind,

but will you officially tell the staff? Otherwise it will
seem 'Mrs. Rafe is puttin' 'erself forward!'"

When I told Ludo the new arrangement, his blue
eyes were strangely blank. "Darling, you *do* want me to
finish the book?" He nodded emphatically. "Well, then
—I have to concentrate, which I can't if I'm also being
the fountainhead for domestic relations. Isn't it more
sensible for Helen to take over, since she's here? She
can fit it with looking for a house; I simply *can't* fit it
with African legends."

"So you've turned your sister-in-law into a superior
housekeeper?"

I felt a bit anxious at this reaction. "Should I *not*
have asked her? Perhaps you'd rather I hired someone? But it's only a few months till I'm finished, and
truly she didn't seem to mind."

"I'm certain she didn't," he said dryly, turning to his
dressing room.

"But you'd *rather* I did it myself," I stated bluntly.
"All right, darling. I'll tell her not to bother, after all."

His hand on the doorknob, he said slowly, "No, by
all means, make use of Helen to spare yourself. You
were a clever puss to have thought of it." He chuckled
reflectively, swinging open the door and looking back
at me.

That was when he said, "Bianca beloved, you are a
genius of absurdity and more fun than people." He
threw back his head and laughed deeply . . . but I
was still anxious. Did he, or did he not, really approve?
We were still, I thought, at the stage of marriage where
each tries sincerely to agree, to please, the other. It's
not easy to adjust two humans to run tandem. The first
year sets habits: who gives in first, has what small
idiosyncracy—and it's more important to identify what
irritates than what pleases.

Was Ludo irritated with me? His eyes focussed in a
brilliant blue flash. "I adore you," he said quietly.
"You are the light of my life, my joy forever. Your

mind is as clear as a cool mountain stream, your tongue as honest as noon sunlight, your heart as loving as Psyche." He grinned wickedly. "I must not really have been such a bastard as everyone thought," he remarked, "to reap a reward like you, my sweet!"

So Helen ran the house while I finished the book, and we worked out the entertainment schedule in perfect harmony. Nearly all our friends were in common, after all; rare that we'd give a big party and exclude Rafe and Helen—patently *silly* for them to entertain at restaurants when I wasn't using the dining room. When Ludo was away, we said, "In or out tonight?" and if it was opera or symphony subscription, Helen would ask, "D'you terribly much mind if I ask the Rolands spur-of-the-moment?" Why should I mind? The servants were *there;* if I weren't using them, why not Helen?

"What doing?" Ludo asked, coming panther-footed from his dressing room to kiss me, peering over my shoulder.

"Figuring Helen's bill," I said absently. "How much is nine and seven?"

"Sixteen. Helen's *bill?*"

"For food and liquor," I nodded, industriously totting up under my breath. "There! I suppose it's inaccurate; I never could add—but what's a few pennies? It's all in the family." Glancing into the mirror I caught his face off-guard staring at the account sheet. I couldn't interpret the sardonic tilt of his eyebrows. "We agreed she'd pay for supplies for their friends. Should I not have asked it? I thought reimbursing us would be less than a restaurant—and so much more pleasant," I faltered. "When I'll be out anyway, why should the servants sit on their duff?"

"Why, indeed," he agreed, straightening up. "And have you had a check from Helen?"

I stared at him. "Of course. She forgot the first

month because she was so busy with that Charity Ball, but when Miss English came to balance my books, I went up and reminded her."

"Mmmmm, and . . . ?"

"She wrote a check; she hasn't forgotten since. After all, I can't be going upstairs like a *landlady* or something," I pointed out. "That was why this whole thing started in the first place, so I wouldn't be interrupted, so everything would run on greased wheels."

"That it does," he murmured, but his expression was still—peculiar. "Binks, you and Helen get along well?"

"Heavens, yes! I'll miss her dreadfully when they move," I told him earnestly. "I never had a sister, you know. It's so pleasant to have someone to laugh and chat with."

Ludo pulled me up into his arms, to kiss me leisurely and thoroughly, than which there was no whicher in my book. Snuggled against him, with his chin resting atop my head, I really was out of this world—hugging a secret that needed another month to be sure . . . but Ludo was still strange. "You know so much," he murmured, as if to himself, "and so little . . ."

I never had any problems with the servants; they seemed all genuinely to like me, to be pleased the Master was finally married and happy. The sole reservation was Victor.

He was a small swarthy Italian Ludo'd acquired in a fracas in Singapore, where Victor'd somehow been hit on the head, rolled, and left behind when the freighter on which he'd signed weighed anchor. Ludo came along at the psychological moment when Victor was embroiled with the gendarmerie for trying to filch some *chupattis*, and when Ludo addressed him in Italian, Victor broke into tears. They'd been together ever since, and Victor was literally Ludo's slave.

It was not hatred, nor dislike, merely a faint reserve. He was unfailingly polite, meticulous in obey-

ing any instruction, but there was always a Berlin
Wall of formality. "He feels left out," Ludo grinned,
waggling his eyebrows salaciously.

"You used to go wenching together?" I asked, and
at Ludo's shout of laughter, "What's so funny? Of
course he's at loose ends with you gone respectable.
We'd better get him a wife, too. How about Esther?"

He stopped laughing and looked at me thoughtfully.
"Do you think you can?"

"Very easily," I assured him, "unless Victor can't
stand her. Otherwise she's panting to be asked! Your
job is (a) suggest the concept of marriage, (b) em-
phasize the delights of permanency, and (c) why not
Esther?"

"You could bend the Devil himself to your will,"
Ludo remarked a month later.

"What *do* you mean?"

"We are invited to a wedding. Victor and Esther
would be deeply flattered if we would attend them."

"Oh, *yes!* Isn't it wonderful? We bought her wedding dress yesterday, at Bendel's," I said enthusiasti-
cally. "What are you giving Victor?"

"What would you suggest?" Ludo asked expressionlessly.

"Two weeks on the boat in Trinidad, if you could do
without him? We'll be here for Christmas, after all,
and you won't need the boat."

"Have you any idea of the cost?"

"Oh, *thousands,* I expect," I said placidly, "but the
boat costs even when it's sitting still, doesn't it? And
you're rich—and Esther's never been *anywhere*—and
Victor's more or less your familiar, isn't he? And we
want them to be happy as we are, so why not start
them off with a bang?"

"Oh, wise young judge!" he murmured, incredulously. "What in hell did I do before I had you, Bi?"

"Oh, you got along," I remarked calmly, "as well
as a short—to say nothing of redheads, blondes and

piebald. I often wonder how you bear this constant diet of brunette."

"It was always my favorite dish," he assured me, "but somehow the seasoning is more subtle, the stuffing more varied."

So that was when I told him. "You made this particular stuffing, darling. I must say, I wonder what's in it . . ."

For a brief moment I thought his face looked like Joseph in one of the old monastery manuscripts: illuminated—but I was always fanciful.

"A roulette wheel: my red, your black," he said, and swung me into his arms bodily. "Oh, Bi, dearest —*when?*" It was the sort of shining awed moment that must be taken lightly, or there will be too much emotion.

"Mid-June—shall we sell chances on the day and hour? Put the money in a college fund? Unless you think it'll grow up to be a croupier?"

"Dos á cheval," Perryn commented, when Ludo formally announced my delicate condition on Christmas Eve, "and what about double zero?"

"DeCourcy twins!" Rafe raised his glass unsteadily. "Here's to a full basket!" he said, tossing off the wine and lurching forward to kiss me heartily, while Ludo squinched his eyes at me proudly.

"*I* shall learn to knit," Helen announced regally, and at the burst of laughter, looked from one to another of us, slightly affronted. "What's so funny? It's the measure of my devotion to Bi that I'm willing to make one of those earnest females sitting around the knitting counter at Bloomingdale's."

"You're bound to come out with a patterned ski sweater," Perryn said when he'd stopped laughing. "Make it a size 38, so it won't be a total loss, Nell, sweetie?"

Every Christmas was happy, but that was the happiest, when for the first time we were a complete *family*, with gaily wrapped parcels piled high beneath a tree that was so tall Victor'd had to lop off the topmost branches—his first chore after the honeymoon. It was a tree we trimmed ourselves, like kids, on Christmas Eve . . . with Ludo precariously perched on the cellar stepladder, and all of us holding our breath, bracing the thing against his six-foot-four two hundred pounds.

But he *would*, personally, as Head of the House of Trael, fasten the little angel to the top. Heavens, I was glad to get him down again in one piece, and never mind how big a piece he was! Perryn did the rest of the upper branches: tall, slim, a carbon copy of Ludo —the same russet hair, piercing blue eyes, the same swashbuckling air. Helen said they looked like old Ludo, so presumably Rafe resembled his DeCourcy mother, with dark French eyes and fine-boned suavity. Privately, he was my concept of Cardinal Richelieu.

"Next year," I said gaily, "we can trim *two* trees: one here and one in your own home."

"What *are* you talking about?" Rafe's eyes were blank.

"I've found the perfect place for you and Helen," I told him triumphantly. There was a long silence, until Ludo said quietly, standing just behind me, "When, where, tell us, tell us all about it, Bi."

"This afternoon! I'd been getting a last-minute present, and of course there *weren't* any taxis, so I took a Third Avenue bus—which is why we never realized, because we never go that way—but there's a new apartment building! *Right* on our own street, only two blocks away—and that was one big problem always, for us to be very near, wasn't it?"

"Yes, *yes*, it was," Helen agreed breathlessly. "Oh, *me*! I never thought to look so far east . . ."

"So I went in and asked—and there's a duplex penthouse," I said impressively. "Four bedrooms and baths on top, *with* individual terraces—one for Rafe's study, you see? And on the lower floor: an immense living room with fireplace, a dining room (I think it's bigger than ours!), a library—huge pantry, modern kitchen, butler's room with bath . . . servants' quarters in the basement, however many you need if you want live-in help."

"What other kind?" Rafe's eyes flickered oddly as he turned to refill the brandy glass. "What else, Bi?"

"Garage in the building, of course—huge terraces running completely around the main floor, with an unobstructed view of the river . . . but best of all: they're precisely at the stage where you can alter, tell them what you want and they'll finish to suit you. No expensive alterations, you see? No waiting around while somebody rips out a wall or puts in a closet," I looked at Helen proudly. "So many places you found needed more remodelling than they were worth, remember?"

"A co-op," I take it?" Ludo inquired. "Did you think to ask how much, Bi?"

I grinned at him wickedly. "For once I remembered something! A hundred thousand, a thousand a month to carry, which includes three servants' rooms and garage service—but if you get a butler-chauffeur, I don't think you'd need more than a cook and two maids, do you?"

Ludo's impassivity creased into silent laughter. "That's a question for Helen, not me," he protested, dropping a fleeting kiss on my forehead. "Well, you were a clever puss to have found the very place!" He threw an arm about my shoulder and turned to Rafe. "It seems, brother, that at long last you'll have your own household."

"Hadn't *we* better see the place?" Rafe said plaintively. "Not that I doubt Bi's judgment."

"Of course," Ludo agreed heartily, "but from Bi's description, it's exactly what you wanted, particularly if you can specify finishing to suit yourselves. How long before occupancy, Binks?"

"A month, depending on what you want—but you have to furnish and get servants." I looked at Helen. "I don't see how you can do it that soon," I said affectionately, "except I'll do dull things like dishtowels, and pots and pans, but I think you can't plan for less than three full months."

"Which brings us to April Fool's Day before we'll lose you, brother," Ludo commented regretfully, "by which time we'll all have adjusted to the loss."

"I hope I can manage it in such a short time," Helen murmured uneasily. Her eyes were oddly half-frightened as she glanced at Rafe. I thought I understood; she'd never had to buy furnishings, was uncertain about her ability to satisfy Rafe's taste—and I already knew privately that he could be *un peu difficile,* and that Helen loved him as I loved Ludo.

"Where's the rush? You want the place to be perfect, but once you *have* it, what difference does it make when you actually move in?" I smiled encouragingly at Helen. "*Heavens,* we're going to have fun!"

"That sounds ominous for the bank account," Perryn observed. "Two women let loose in New York shops? What one can't think of, the other will!" He laughed infectiously, while Rafe tossed off his *fine.* "I say, stop hogging the brandy," he protested. "Fill up all around, Rafe, so we can drink to the newest Trael establishment."

"Of course, sorry . . ." Rafe rapidly filled four snifters, handing them around. Extending a glass to me, he smiled crookedly. "To you first, Bi! All these months Helen's been tramping about town—and you look at just one place, and it's the right one. That's the devil's own luck!"

"So my wife is smarter than yours, brother," Ludo said smoothly, raising his glass, and smiling down at me intently. "I'll drink to the innocent heart, the loving fondness, of my wife!" I could feel myself blushing with confusion; these were the sort of words Ludo usually only used in private . . . but he was a bit above himself that night because of the Announcement to come.

"To Bi!" they chorused solemnly, and Perryn added, "the clever puss!" Everybody sipped formally, but Rafe drained his glass and refilled, ignoring Helen's troubled eyes.

"Now—to Rafe and Helen, and the loveliest home in the world," Ludo smiled directly at Helen. "You've waited a long while, Nell—been a very good girl, think I don't know? You deserve the best there is!"

For a moment, Helen's face crumpled defenselessly; almost, I thought she was going to cry when we toasted her, but she pulled herself together, with a swift glance at Rafe that ended in contemplation of her toes. "I already have the best there is," she said, and tossed off the remainder of her brandy.

"Hey, aren't I anything?" Perryn asked, aggrieved.

"Of course!" I was a bit flown with brandy myself at that point. "To our sister-in-law-to-come—poor child! But at least she'll make the Sextette from Lucia . . ."

"If he remembers to get a singer," Ludo remarked, "but somehow, I think he'll have other requirements. To Perryn!"

"If it's my future wife, I can drink too!" Perryn drained his glass with a laugh, and extended it for a refill that emptied the decanter. "Send for another bottle, old boy," he told Ludo. "We haven't finished with the tree, what with all this excitement and it is obviously going to be An Evening."

So Victor brought another bottle, and Helen and I finished the lower branches, while the men sat in a row over the brandy, like Edwardian bucks at The Gaiety—making faintly indecent remarks as we nipped up and down the stepladder . . . until we were all helpless with laughter . . . until I remembered Gilbert & Sullivan: "It's a rule for all family fools, if a joke is too French, half a crown's stopped out of your wages," I stated coldly. Perryn choked on his drink, swallowed the wrong way and gasped miserably for several minutes while Rafe and Ludo banged his shoulders with more good will than judgment.

"Oh, are we going *French?*" Helen inquired, picking up her long velvet skirts and essaying a few discreet can-can kicks.

"Higher!" the men commanded, settling back in their chairs.

Helen eyed them austerely. "Not without pants," she said, and turned back to the tree with a flirt of her tail.

"Bi?"

"I don't wear 'em either."

"All the better!" Rafe said loudly. "Eh, brothers?"

I shook my head. "You have to pay to see what I've got, darlings!" Very deliberately and seductively, I wound up for a grind and bump I'd learned from a Sorbonne classmate who was putting herself through classes by a strip-act in Pigalle. It was a *sensational* success. Perryn tipped his chair backward, landing on the floor with long legs waggling wildly in the air. . . . Ludo laughed until he was wiping his eyes . . . Rafe held up the brandy bottle. "Brother, she's worth paying for," he stated, indistinctly. "Take off your shoes, Bi, so we can drink from 'em."

"Bi—Bi—Baby!" Perryn added, rolling lithely from the overturned chair and pulling himself to his feet, just as Victor and Esther appeared with supper.

Oh, we were all tiddly, but it was more happiness than alcohol. We made Victor and Esther bring plates and glasses for themselves. "You're part of the family, *heavens*, you're both senior to me!" Perryn loaded the phonograph; everybody danced with everybody else, and it was the most delicious Welsh Rarebit I ever ate —until suddenly the records clicked to a stop, and the great-grandfather clock rang midnight in the still-ness.

"I've a Christmas present to share with all of you," Ludo said deeply.

Perryn straightened up, holding the records against his chest. Rafe's hand held the wine bottle suspended with Helen curved within his other arm. Victor set the dirty plates on the tray with the slightest *chink* and turned to stand formally, with Esther beside him.

"Next year there'll be more of us," said Ludo, sim-ply. "Bianca's having a baby."

What I remember best about that moment is the half-envious eyes of Helen and Esther, before the hubbub of Perryn's gleeful shout, Rafe's hug and kiss, Victor's polite "Congratulations, madame!" But his eyes were warmly approving for the first time, and somehow I had a suspicion. "*Fortuna grande,*" I mur-mured and was certain from the twinkle of his eyes.

"Twins it'll be—one of each," Perryn chortled, splashing brandy over his ruffled dinner shirt with a dramatic gesture. "I speak for the boy," he cried. "I'll forswear the Devil for him on your behalf, Bil'"

But of course I never do anything right.

I managed to drop the basket three months later. It was twins, both boys. If I could have hung onto them just two weeks more, modern medicine would have saved at least one.

Helen felt almost worse than I. "I can't—ever," she said, starkly. "I thought—you go away so often, you'd certainly leave the babies with me, rather than a hired nurse. I was *so* looking forward to it," she whispered.

"There'll be other babies," I comforted, but appar-ently it wasn't going to be that easy.

"I blame myself severely," Dr. Raymond said. "Mrs.

Trael will always be a Caesarean, but I should not have taken any chances with twins."

"You mean Bi—Mrs. Trael—ought not to have children?" Ludo asked harshly.

"Not at all, but it will require care," Dr. Raymond said comfortably. "Always a Caesar, and probably seven months because of that tiny pelvis—but nothing to worry about."

"What'n hell are you talking about?" Ludo demanded, white-faced. "D'you think I'd take any chance at all—*with Bi?*"

"Oh, don't be silly, darling," I said impatiently. "When should I start again?"

"Six months—a year would be better, you're young enough." He pursed his lips, standing up. "A preparatory diet and exercises . . . why not come in to see me when you're ready?"

"Of course, and thanks so much, Dr. Raymond."

"Why did you thank him?" Ludo demanded when the door closed.

"Well, I'm not dead, am I?"

"No, and you never will be!"

That was the only near-fight we ever had; it continued off and on for months. Basically it was: "I want your baby," versus, "I want you!"

"Don't press him too hard," Dr. Raymond advised. "Let him think you're resigned and leave the rest to Dame Nature. She has a way of working things out." He smiled, standing up and extending his hand across the desk. "You're in good physical shape," he said quietly. "We know the technical problems now, but there's nothing to worry about. I confess," he narrowed his eyes, holding my hand gently, "I'd be happier if— wherever you are when you find yourself pregnant again, you'd make tracks for home and me—perhaps that's only my egotism—but don't worry, next time we'll pull it off!"

* * *

There never was a next time.

There never would be, now . . .

In the dimness of the suite, I twisted my hands together and writhed on the couch. If only I'd had a child—but if it were a son, Ludo'd have taken him as ruthlessly as he'd taken everything else.

I rolled over and up to my feet. *No use to think about might have beens* . . . I was alone and friendless—unless I could still talk to Helen?

I hadn't seen her since that dreadful day. We'd spoken once, the day I was packing, waiting for Railway Express. "Binks?" her voice was hushed, secretive. "Oh, sweetie—what'n hell is going on?"

"Why ask me? I'm whistling in the dark."

"Listen, I don't dare talk for long—Rafe would *kill* me . . ."

I melted at once; she was still my friend, willing to risk displeasure to make a phone call—and I could imagine exactly how Rafe had laid down the law!" "It's wonderful to hear your voice," I said shakily. "I'm completely at sea—except Ludo's thrown me out on my ear. I'll be gone tomorrow—and I still haven't the faintest idea *why?* Helen, if you love me—for God's sake find out from Rafe?"

"Don't you suppose I asked?" she countered. "He didn't say a word that made sense, Binks . . . just forbade me ever to see or talk to you again." She caught her breath, anguished. "We're having to move back there as soon as you've gone . . . sell this place . . . oh, Binks!"

Even in the midst of my own anguish I could share her tears. For months, we'd ranged about New York together and separately, finding this and that to turn Mrs. Ralph Trael's penthouse apartment into a ten-page photographic spread in *Town & Country*. At first she was oddly price-conscious, hesitant over even such staples as beds and sheets, until I protested mildly. "Darling, these one must have . . ."

"I know." She clenched her hands together tightly and turned to me. "But I can't afford them," she said starkly. "Don't you understand? Rafe bought the apartment, but that's only the beginning. We didn't have *anything;* it means thousands more for everything, down to the last wastebasket." Her voice trailed away tiredly. "I haven't got it, Binks."

"I have," I said, quietly. "Oh, sweetie, forgive me! I never thought! I knew how you wanted a home of your own, and *stupid me,* I didn't think of what extras there'd be. "No," as she opened her mouth, "not to say a *word!* My present, please? Let's say twenty thousand for wastebaskets?"

We weren't kissing women, Helen and I. She looked at me for a moment, and held out her hand. "D'you know what you're doing?" she said in an undertone.

I could see tears in the corners of her eyes. "Yes," I said lightly, "I'm buying my way into interior decoration. *Heavens,* won't it be *fun* to make a home—even if it isn't mine . . ."

Ludo was away six weeks (when he got back I knew he'd been to Madagascar by the heavenly tourmalines he'd brought me: all shades of green with pink and blue tinges), but with the book finished at last, I had plenty of time on my hands. Helen and I were out and around every day, and gradually the apartment took shape. It ran more than twenty thousand, of course. Helen's taste was impeccable, and once we'd embarked on the job, it was obviously absurd to compromise. "Why ruin the ship for a ha'p'orth of tar?" I said lightly. "And I've just got my next quarter's allowance, so let's do it *right?*"

Then the very day they moved in, and Ludo came home, I was dropping the basket, so there was never a housewarming, after all. It had all to be cancelled, and some guests didn't get the message in time and turned up in white tie and diamonds, to be told, "Mr. Trael's apologies, but there is illness in the family." Perryn had flown over from Gstaad specially, too—although when they let him in to see me, he said taut-jawed, "Don't you know I'd have come at once anyway? Thank God I was on the spot, instead of chewing my nails on a plane!" He glared at Ludo across the hospital bed. "And where were you when the lights went out?" he demanded. "Dammit, you don't deserve her!"

"No," Ludo said calmly, "but praise the Lord, I've got a second chance."

"I'm glad I'm so precious, but do you mind not fighting over me here?" I murmured plaintively. "There's not enough space. Why not go into the hall and settle it? The winner can come back . . ."

"Murderess!" Perryn remarked with a grin. "As if I were ever up to Ludo's weight . . ." He leaned over to kiss me heartily. "Get well!" he ordered. "I shall stay until you get out of here—and may I remind you, I am missing the best skiing weather?"

Well, I was home within five days—but I never forgave myself for ruining Helen's first big party. She made light of it. "Heavens, what's one more party?" but after thirteen years in someone else's home, I knew how much she must have looked forward to the moment of exhibiting *her* home, *her* taste—and I'd killed it.

"Will you stop mourning?" Rafe said lightly. "It was going to be a total dud; we'd asked all the Old Guard—and if anything, you spared us a dreary evening, if you can bear to look on the bright side."

"So I'm an oboe," I shrugged, and catching the nurse's blank expression, "an ill wind nobody blows good," I explained, but she'd evidently never heard of this.

"Are you chilly, Mrs. Trael?" she asked anxiously, bustling forward with an extra blanket.

"No, just silly," said Ludo. "I think that will be all for the moment, nurse . . ."

We were *just* able to restrain ourselves until she'd closed the door . . .

Five-thirty—Helen might be home, dressing for dinner. I reached for the phone, gave her private number, and luck was with me; she answered at once, with a faint scream at my voice. "Where *are* you?" she said swiftly. "I worried and worried, and nobody knew."

"Room 1022 St. Regis. Couldn't you possibly sneak over for an hour?" I said urgently. "My brother's gone; I'm alone."

"I'll try," her voice dropped to a whisper. "I don't know if I can get out before Rafe gets back."

"Come to the suite, 1020. Oh, Helen, it was all a lie. Those pictures—they weren't me!"

"Yes, I know they weren't," she said unexpectedly. "Oh, *God,* what a mess—I have to hang up, someone's coming . . ." The phone went dead, but I felt a bit cheered. At least, Helen believed me; she'd promised to try to see me. I replaced the phone and sat back on the couch, absently watching the reflection of neon flashes from the street against my window panes. It would be thirty minutes before she could get here . . .

I awoke to the sound of broken glass. How long had I dozed? Groggily, I switched on a lamp and peered at my watch: eight-thirty! Three hours since Helen had said she'd come if she could. Had I slept through her rap on the door, or had she been unable to slip away before Rafe's return? My heart sank. No use to expect her now; they'd be in the middle of the evening's engagement, whatever it was. Tomorrow morning she'd surely manage it—but it was a long time to wait.

Dully, I pulled myself from the couch and went to the door from the suite to my bedroom. It was locked—and that was all of a piece with everything, I thought angrily. We'd had that door opened so I needn't go into the outer hall to reach my room, needn't run any risk of being seen and recognized— and the instant Julian paid the bill and checked out, they locked the door again. Damn them, did I even have the hall key for 1022? I could hear dim sounds from my room—the maid with fresh towels. Furiously I rattled the doorknob and rapped on the panel.

"Open this door *at once!*"

There was no answer; the sounds ceased, and faintly I heard a closing door—the maid, leaving. *Damn the girl* . . . I ran to the door of the suite, flung it open and peered into the hall. It was empty, the service door settling into place, so she'd gone heaven knew where. *Oh, hell!* I found my handbag and temperishly upended it on the couch; at least I did have my key. Stuffing everything back pell-mell, what I didn't have was a key for the suite—and I wouldn't be able to open the connecting door, meaning I'd be locked out of the living room. Well, there was nothing in the suite of value; I snicked the latch and left the door open while I went along the corridor to my room.

I opened the door on total darkness, *reeking* of Nuit de Noel, which was quite simply explained when my hand found the light switch: the broken bottle lay on its side in a puddle of perfume. What was *not* explained and in fact inexplicable, was the total disorder of my room.

Someone had been there, and it was not the maid. Someone had locked the connecting door while I dozed on the couch. Someone had searched wildly, frantically, swiftly, and broken a bottle of perfume in the process. *That* was the tinkle of glass ringing in my ears as I woke—and I had nearly caught whoever it was. What would have happened if, instead of rapping vainly on the locked door, I had instantly

gone to the hall and *seen* someone emerging from
1022?

Then I would have known my enemy.

And my enemy would have known that I knew . . .

I closed and bolted the door with a shiver, leaning
shakily against it while my eyes absorbed open draw-
ers and closet, clothes tumbled on the floor, suitcases
disarranged. Who was searching for what? I had
nothing but essential clothing; all my private papers
and possessions had been sent to storage in Julian's
house.

What did someone think I had that must be retrieved in stealth? No common thief, I felt certain;
Ludo'd stripped me of furs and jewels, but there were
a few family pins and rings from my mother; no hotel
burglar would overlook them, despite their lack of
value. All were in my jewelry box.

Had Ludo commissioned someone to retrieve my
emerald ring, thinking perhaps I might no longer be
wearing it? But the connecting door had been locked
—because it had been stealthily opened for a peek
that showed I was asleep on the couch *with the ring
on my finger!* So it wasn't the ring, but what? The
wildest disorder was my dispatch case—ruthlessly upended on the bed, papers in every direction.

The room had only been searched, I realized as I
moved around picking up dresses, straightening
papers. Nothing had been taken; I didn't think my
jewelry box had even been opened, because every
ring, pin, chain, was exactly as I'd left it. Gradually,
bewilderment became active fear, mingled with doubt.
Was Ludo my enemy, or was there someone else? If
I'd identified that person, would he have killed me
to prevent disclosure?

I could feel my heart pounding in terror. It was
simply *all too much.* I threw everything into my cases,
turned off the lights and rang for an elevator. The

lobby was clear of reporters. I paused briefly at the desk. "I'm checking out; Dr. Robinson paid the bill." A bellboy set my luggage in a cab, and as it drew away from the curb, I said, "LaGuardia, please."

I'd missed the nine o'clock; I was too early for the ten o'clock shuttle, but at least there'd be lights and people. For the first time in my life, I went into a bar unescorted and ordered a highball. The bartender's name was embroidered on his jacket: Sal. The assistant was a large moon-faced man with a bald spot; according to his jacket his name was Sonny. I had time to notice such details, as well as to remember I'd had no dinner. There'd be no food in the house, but I could probably get a sandwich in Washington, if I were hungry. At the moment I wondered if I'd ever feel like eating again.

The bar was fairly crowded, but aside from a couple of Naval ensigns, who eyed me appreciatively, I seemed unnoticed. Nor did any of the people coming into the place after me appear suspicious, as though perhaps they were following me. Slowly, my heart-beat steadied. The bar mirror gave me a clear picture of everyone in the outer waiting room; no face was familiar. I couldn't quite laugh at my panicked flight from the hotel, but I began to feel my fears were overly fanciful. Someone wanted something—but it wasn't my life, or I'd be lying dead in the suite right this minute. Once I left New York, I'd leave my enemy behind; once in Chevy Chase, I might be able to find an answer to this puzzle.

The plane was only half-filled; I had a window seat to myself, the flight was perfectly smooth. Almost before I realized it, we were landing at National Airport. I picked up my suitcases, tucked the attache case under my arm, and found a taxi. Near midnight I was standing before Julian's home. It was dark and silent in the street lights filtering through the new-leafed trees.

There were no lights in any nearby houses, only a few upper-story lights down the block. I had a throb of anxiety. "Please, wait till I've got the door open?"

"Sure, lady," he said in surprise, "but it's real safe out here."

"Yes, but it's my brother's house, and I have to be sure I can make the key work properly."

He brought the cases up to the door, and focussed a flashlight on the lock until I'd found the right key. The door swung open quietly. "You're okay now," he said cheerfully. "Good night, miss," and went back to his cab, while I fumbled for a hall switch. Behind me the cab slid away down the street. I picked up the suitcases and stepped over the threshold, closing the door quietly.

It was a perfectly *horrid* house. It didn't like me, and I didn't like it. I thumped the bags on the floor and spoke to the silence. "I don't want to be here any more than you want to have me—but I've no place else to go," I could feel tears again, "and I'm frightened, and we just have to put up with each other for a while."

Then I sat down on the bottom step of the nasty little staircase and bawled, until the grandfather clock struck twelve, very slowly, pontifically, and off-key, when I sat up and thought distractedly, "Oh, heavens, I'd forgotten you. Now I have to get used to you all over again."

Because that was the ancestral Robinson clock, circa 1790. Before mother died I'd been able to sleep through the hourly chimes; afterwards it was Julian's pride and joy—but I'd been away at school or college, or staying with him and Polly wherever they were. Then I was married. I hadn't heard Grandpa in fifteen years, and listening to the placid tick-tock reverberating through the silence, I thought *If I never heard you again, hello!*

Eventually, I pulled myself from the step, and felt my way upstairs. All the mattresses were neatly rolled on edge for airing, except a couch on what seemed to be an unheated enclosed side porch. It was deathly cold, but there were blankets stacked atop. I unfolded three of them, turned off the lights, kicked off my shoes and lay down, pulling the blankets up to my chin.

The hell with searching for sheets, the hell with undressing, the hell with everything—including me . . .

Chapter
3

Even by daylight, it was still a horrid house, although I sensed a certain slackening in the air, as if it were waiting to see what I'd do but was not wholly unreceptive. About houses I am *not* fanciful. Anyone knows some houses like people and some don't, depending on who's lived in them. Poor things, they're absolutely defenseless against abuse, except to draw into themselves and exude unfriendliness.

After I'd made a complete tour I knew it was only reserved because nobody had ever *loved* it. Privately, I felt it wasn't very lovable in the first place; whoever built the place had lacked imagination, which was undoubtedly why it had appealed instantly to Julian and Polly. The rooms were small and awkward; closets stuck out like afterthoughts, and *all* the floors tilted to the left.

There was a master bedroom, a guest room and a minuscule study containing Julian's desk, with a central bathroom that lacked a shower—and apparently *all* the pipes were furred. "Roto*root*er," said my mind, frivolously. There was the unheated space over the porch, where I'd slept. It seemed to be an extension of Julian's study, crammed with metal files and a drafting board.

That was upstairs. On the main floor there was a living room with fireplace on one side of the entrance hall, and a dining room with an air conditioner on the other side. There was a kitchen, a loo with a slanting ceiling under the stairs that would be instant murder for anything taller than a pygmy, and an afterthought jutting into the backyard pretending to be a pantry.

There was an outdoor thermometer fixed to the window frame of the downstairs loo. It was on the wrong side, so that if one opened the window, the gauge swung unreadably back toward the kitchen door—and was neatly poised to whack anyone coming out.

There was a garage . . . down four steps from the kitchen door and past a high lattice covered with honeysuckle that concealed trash cans, thence to a consciously coy curved path of sham flagstones. A flight of open steps with a single handrail led from kitchen to cellar, which held washer-drier, coalbin and furnace. My personal effects had arrived, and now sat unhappily in a corner, blocking locked cabinets—presumably containing Polly's household treasures. I was inspecting the tightly sealed cartons and valises that held the remains of my life when there was a subterranean rumble.

I swung about, nervously, to observe a side slot of the furnace swinging up to admit a shoveful of anthracite bits to its maw, where it chewed them up voraciously in a shower of sparks, and settled down to a happy hum. Good. I wouldn't have to stoke a furnace, and it could still be chilly, requiring a bit of heat.

The cellar was even drearier than the rest of the house. There were six half-windows; three were cracked and there was an ovoid gobbet fallen out of one over the coal bin. I turned on my heel and went back to the kitchen, which was the best place in the house. Poor Polly, her only passion (aside from Julian) was gourmetise. I visualized her *planning* this kitchen: using every inch to advantage, hanging the shining pots, the kitchen tools from pegboard, with a window

tray that was barren now but must have been meant
for fresh chives and basil.

I looked around—at the filthy pans, dull copper.
The tenants had obviously been pigs, and thank good-
ness Polly couldn't see her adored kitchen. The re-
frigerator had been turned off, of course; I turned it
on again, suppressing a shudder at the congealed slops
and spills festooning the inside. Time enough to clean
thoroughly later—what else did I have but time?

In a way, the nastiness of the house was *cheering*.

Nothing is more therapeutic to a woman than house-
cleaning. I hadn't so much as looked at a stove or
sink in more than four years, and I was never more
domestic than required for subsistence, yet faced with
dirt, I was instantly a woman.

The pantry shelves yielded a cupful of flour (wee-
villy), a few tablespoons of sugar, half a can of olive
oil (rancid) and a quarter jar of instant coffee. Well,
what more could any red-blooded American woman
wish than a cup of coffee?

I carried it with me, sipping leisurely, on a second
inspection trip from top to bottom. I found linen in
a huge mock-Sheraton chest. I set down the coffee
cup, and unrolled the mattresses energetically. I made
all the beds, put towels on the bathroom racks, plus a
fresh cake of soap and loo tissue—by which time the
coffee was stone cold, of course.

I went downstairs and made a fresh cup, jotting
notes on a pad disinterred from my dispatch case.
Food and cleaning supplies—introduce myself to the
bank and put away the emerald. I was still sure it
was not the object of search, but better be safe than
sorry, and I'd promised Julian, anyway.

Rinsing out the cup and setting it in the drainer, I
felt a change in the atmosphere. It was still a horrid
house, but somehow, now, it was half-apologetic, half-
hopeful, as if to say "I can't help the way I look—but
perhaps you'll *do* something?"

I felt a bit apologetic myself; no amount of money could ever give charm or personality to this place. It was born to be an ugly duckling, and aside from the kitchen, Polly was no help. Every room was papered; every room was *green*— from immense cabbage roses on black-green for the dining room, to itty-bitty daisies on Nile green for the master bedroom. Julian's study was a modern design of orange cubes and shocking pink rhomboids scattered over a shade only to be termed expectant mother green—which, if you'd never met Polly but only knew she had seven children, might have seemed a subtlety.

But I did know Polly, and she was *perfect* for Julian. Neither would have seen an innuendo even if it were illustrated in Fabulous Cinemascope with a score by Tiomkin. Polly was good, Polly was earnest from the top of her Boston hat to the tips of her sensible walking shoes. She'd never complained when I was dumped on her, here or there at various stations around the world during my school days. She was always either "quickening" or had just dropped the basket, so presumably I'd never seen her at her best, but as Ludo said, "What'n hell else is there to *do* in up-country Borneo—and servants are a dime a dozen."

Looking at Polly's home, I realized it had never been meant for anything but Julian's retirement. Not enough room for children—and nothing beyond the bare necessities of furnishings. Here and there I recognized bits of family furniture inherited from mother; the interstices were filled with cheap makeshifts. I wondered why they'd bought so long before Julians' three score and five—except it might be cheaper to store the good stuff in his own home rather than a warehouse, and let the rent carry the place?

Eventually I took my shopping list to the garage, found a map in the glove compartment of the Volkswagen, and plotted a route to civilization. I located the bank and introduced myself to Lennart as Dr.

Robinson's sister. He was a string bean with teeth, and he assumed I was Miss Robinson. Why correct him? I rented a box and set my rings therein; I signed for a checking account and deposited Julian's money.

There was a Safeway across the street; I laid in a complete supply of food and cleaning aids. On impulse, I bought three packets of nasturtium seeds and a bag of fertilizer. I'd seen some sort of flower bed as I went to the garage. After I'd lugged all the paper sacks into the kitchen, I investigated. It was a rose garden, with two dozen bushes, all showing signs of life. I looked at them dubiously. I am no gardener, but I distinctly recalled hearing that roses are extremely *fussy*.

While I was cogitating, a voice said, "How d'you do? Are you a new tenant? I'm Miss King, two houses down . . ."

Oh dear, one of the neighbors I mustn't get chummy with . . . not that anyone would have wished to chum with Miss King, when I looked at her. *Genus gossip* at first sight of the mean little eyes glittering avidly behind thick bifocals . . . "How do you do?" I said, repressively. "I am Dr. Robinson's sister."

"Oh? Oh!" Her voice went up and down, excitedly. "How *nice*! If you'll forgive plain speaking, Miss Robinson, we really did *not* care for the last tenants. Such a *pity* for the neighbors when a house is constantly rented—tenants never take the same pride—depreciates all the other property, you know . . . but of course, entirely different to have you, and when will your brother and sister-in-law be returning? You'll be staying until then, of course?"

"I really don't know, our plans are uncertain." *Detestable* woman; I turned away impersonally. "If you'll excuse me? I have something on the stove . . ."

By the end of the day I'd discovered it wasn't that easy. Life in suburbia is the essence of social blackmail, and for me, it was compounded by the nerves,

the bewilderment, the fear through which I'd passed
in the last few weeks. Each time the doorbell rang,
my heart went up to my throat, and it would be a
second peal before I could force myself to answer.

Apparently news of an outlander spreads through
Chevy Chase more quickly than by African drums—
although I wouldn't put them past Miss King. There
were two youngsters, inquiring about newspaper de-
livery: one for morning, one for evening. There was
a milkman, followed by another milkman from a rival
establishment. There was a cleaner, laundryman, and
a man trying to sell firewood. There was also: the boy
across the street to say he took care of the grounds
and would clip the hedge on Saturday—two little
girls selling chances on a sponge cake to be baked by
someone's mother (I never did find out what this was
in aid of) . . . an earnest young woman, with a spot
of lipstick on her teeth, representing Jehovah's Wit-
nesses, who wished me to sit "at peace in the living
room and seek Jesus together" . . . an insurance man,
asking questions about Julian's former tenants . . . a
man from Goodwill to collect old newspapers, if I
had any . . .

I said "No" to everyone, and just as I was fixing a
well-deserved pre-dinner highball there was a final
ring. I flung open the door with venom trembling on
my lips, to face a small boy, dirty-faced and tear-
stained, holding a black cat uncomfortably draped over
his arms. "Please, would you like a cat?" he asked
tremulously. They both looked at me anxiously. I hesitated, and the child said, "Please, he has to have a
home, because we're going away tomorrow . . . and
he's a very good cat."

"I'm sure he is." Instinctively I reached to pluck
the beast into my arms, where he cuddled against my
shoulder with an almost audible sigh of relief and
began purring like a steam engine. Well, I am a

sucker for cats. "You'd like me to keep him a couple
of weeks till you come back?" I asked.

He shook his head sadly. "We're going to South
Africa for three years," he said, "and if I don't find a
home," he caught his breath, "mother will have to
send him somewhere. *Please?*"

I'm a sucker for little boys, too. "Of *course* I'll take
him! What's his name?"

"Arthur, because he spends nights on the round
table. I think that's a joke, but I don't really understand it," he said honestly. "It's father's joke, actually."

I sat down on the outside steps. "It's a good joke,"
I assured him, straight-faced. "Would you like to say
goodbye to Arthur?" I handed the cat into his pipe-
cleaner arms and averted my eyes from the convulsive
squeeze, the face buried against fur. Faintly a voice
called, "Danny? *Danny!*"

Arthur landed in my arms again. "I have to go,"
Danny said, standing up and looking at me squarely.
"You take care of him, he's a very *good* cat."

"I *promise*," I said firmly. "Thank you for giving
him to me. The one thing I was wanting was a good
cat . . ."

So I had a bundle of black plush sleeping at my
feet each night, and something to talk to during the
day, even if it was a one-way conversation. Danny
was right; Arthur was a *very* good cat. He knew the
locale better than I, and wanted *out* for long hours
every day, but he always came back several times to
reassure me of his well-being. I let my fingers do the
walking through the Yellow Pages and found a pet
supply shop, where I bought him a scarlet collar hung
with bells.

From a gardening book on the shelves, I'd learned
roses require massive doses of fertilizer in spring.

Each afternoon I industriously loosened soil and fed the bushes with Arthur to keep me company.

"Well, I see *you've* got him now," Miss King remarked superciliously. "Three years that beast's been living off the land, but that nine lives adage is certainly true! He always finds an *in* for himself, plus killing all the lovely cardinals and bluejays."

I looked at the nasty little Pekingese yapping hysterically at the end of its leash—and at Arthur's calm demeanor—and said casually, "I doubt he'll catch many birds; I've belled him as you see—and if he does . . . well, frankly, the only thing I detest worse than dogs is a bluejay."

So now I had a feline familiar, plus a rose garden, plus at least one inimical neighbor . . . and two days later I had Peace Beloved.

She arrived at ten in the morning, letting herself in with a key, and humming lightheartedly to the tune on her transistor radio. She was squab-breasted, lightly toasted on all sides, and her IQ was approximately 50—and I may have been overgenerous in my estimate. Leaning over the upper railing, I said, "Who are you—and will you please turn off that damnable noise?"

She squealed wildly, and stared in every direction but up . . . but at least she shut the thing off. "I is Peace Beloved," she quavered. "I goes with the house. They didn't tell me there was new tenants."

"I'm not a tenant, I'm Dr. Robinson's sister." She was still looking about vaguely. "I'm upstairs," I said helpfully. She came forward to the newel post and looked up timidly, her face breaking into a full smile as she caught sight of me at last.

"*There* you is!" she said happily. "Fo' a minute, I couldn't *find* you."

"I'm very much here, I assure you," I told her grimly, "and I regret to say there will be no Beatles within my hearing, you understand?"

She stared at me, obviously in total shock, and popped her gum. It sounded louder than an A-bomb, and Arthur, who'd descended to the landing to reconnoiter, recoiled violently and raced back to the safety of my dressing gown.

"And will you please dispose of that bubble gum before I come down for breakfast?" I asked politely. "Otherwise you're on your own . . ."

"Yas'm," she said faintly, scooping a disgusting gray wad from her mouth.

"Do *not* park it on the bannister," I instructed, and went back to my bedroom, where I eyed the growing pile of soiled underthings. Could I entrust them to this girl? Oh, for Esther! Once married to Victor, she'd quietly but firmly taken over the job of lady's maid. In four years I'd never needed a safety pin, a needle and thread, clean stockings or fresh white gloves. Brushing my long black hair, I stared at myself in the mirror. *This is a bore; why don't I get it cut?*

Well, why not? It was Ludo who'd rhapsodized, luxuriated in my hair, who wouldn't hear of trimming even a few inches to make it more manageable —but there was no more Ludo. I swirled the strands into a pile on top of my head, thrust pins here and there, and went downstairs—to find fresh coffee, orange juice, and hot pancakes slothered with butter and currant jelly.

Peace Beloved's face was so proud that I hadn't the heart to say I never ate much for breakfast. "I couldn't find any syrup," she apologized anxiously. "Does you want eggs, Miss Robinson? I didn't know how you'd like 'em fixed."

"This will be plenty, thanks." The coffee was delicious; the pancakes light as a feather—none of Ludo's chefs could have done better. "I'm as surprised at you as you with me," I said with a smile. "Dr. Robinson was in such a hurry to get back to Venezuela, he simply gave me the keys and never said a word about you. Have you been with them long?"

"Ever since they bought the house. I comes every week to clean and do laundry. Mrs. Robinson ask me to keep an eye on everything for her, make sure tenants don't break too much, or steal things when they leave." She smiled at me broadly. "O'course, you is different. I don't has to watch you," she confided with a chuckle. "You is *family*."

With the coming of Peace Beloved, my home was complete. She might be a total loss for conversation, but her eyes sparkled with pleasurable awe at sight of my laundry. "They's every bit hand-made?" That they were, and they were going to have to last me the rest of my life, but Peace Beloved handled them with gossamer fingers. She was an excellent plain cook, and her cleaning went through the house like a dose of salts.

At five o'clock I asked if she had any free days, which elicited an involved discourse, that, not rightly she didn't, but if I wanted her, she'd turn her clients onto her lazy sister-in-law who didn't want to work *nohow*. I wanted her; she'd come Monday, Wednesday, Friday. Did I want the silver? The family china? These items were in the locked cellar cabinets, but Peace Beloved had a key.

She also knew where Polly traded, the location of a lending library, and the occupant of every house on the block, but unlike Miss King, Peace Beloved's gossip was kindly. Perched on a kitchen stool, she looked wistful as I lit a cigarette. "Would you like one?"

"You doesn't mind? Mrs. Robinson don't let me smoke while I is working." That figured; Polly doesn't smoke, although she considers Julian's cigarettes and pipe "manly."

"I don't mind, so long as you're careful."

Peace Beloved rooted in her capacious bag with a sigh of relief. Her cup of joy was evidently complete, and in the space of two cigarettes, I heard rather more than I wished to learn about my neighbors. The sole exception was the house next door, which was the only other rental on this block. The tenants were named Crosson; he worked for the Government, she was a teacher, and there was a little girl— but not even Miss King had been able to learn anything more. Peace Beloved had once worked for previous tenants and knew the layout of the house, which sounded *big*, but apparently Mrs. Crosson did her own housework.

I finally dismissed her with tactful firmness, or I think she'd have stayed to cook dinner, but as it happens, I am as good a cook as Polly. Surveying the spanking clean kitchen, I mentally rubbed my hands. *Fun* to go through the cookbooks, try some new recipes. Peace Beloved had left the cellar key with me; I had a hunch Polly'd locked away her best equipment. Arthur accompanied me to the basement and prowled about while I dug out a blender and hand mixer. There was a fry kettle, a rotisserie, a fondue set . . . a shelf of tinned delicacies . . .

I had just relocked the cabinet when there was a horrendous avalanche in the coal bin—from whence Arthur emerged with a mouse, to the intense satisfaction of both of us. "Kill it; don't play with it," I commanded, "and then you may eat it *down here!*" I left him masticating blissfully and took Polly's equipment up to the kitchen.

It occurred to me as I sat over Polly's cookbooks that evening: I had a cat, a maid, a rose garden, plenty to read, and a well-stocked liquor cabinet in the cellar, plus a superb kitchen to play in. Later I could drag my typewriter up to Julian's study and try my hand at

writing . . . but aside from necessary directions to
Peace Beloved, there seemed now no reason why I
should be forced to speak to a soul for the next six
months.

It was an immensely comforting thought. Already
the atmosphere of the house was tentatively friendly.
It was still a horrid house, but at least *it* knew I knew
it couldn't help itself. Averting my eyes from the bad
reproduction of those dreary Van Gogh sunflowers
"arting up" the mantel wall, I thought I'd been right
to come here, after all . . .

Chapter
4

In spite of myself, I made one friend. It rained early Saturday, leaving the rose bed exactly right for easy weeding. Arthur and I were crawling around, removing incipient plantains and keeping a weather eye on Miss King's door. We were tacitly agreed: the instant it opened, we returned to the house. There was time to retreat with dignity, as though we were either finished for the day or something was boiling over . . . by which means we'd successfully avoided the old witch for a week.

"That's the very nicest bush," a voice announced behind me, as I dragged the pad along. Turning, I saw a small girl, viewing my labors with approval. "Have you come to live here?" she asked. "Are you going to take care of the roses? The last people *didn't!*"

"I'll be here for a while," I said, amused by her minatory tone. "Who are you?"

"I'm Suzanne Crosson, I'm eight years old, I'm in the fourth grade, I like arithmetic best and I'm no good at spelling," she said rapidly, disposing of all the amenities in one fell swoop. "Who are you?"

"I'm the sister of the man who owns this house, I'm twenty-nine years old, finished with college, and *my* best subject is history," I told her, straight-faced. It seemed a satisfactory biography. Suzanne nodded her head briskly.

"You're pretty," she announced. "Do you like roses?"

"I don't know, I never had any before—and thank you for the compliment."

"You're welcome. You're supposed to bank the earth around the roots. Can I help you weed?"

"By all means, but I haven't another pad; your knees will be filthy," I warned.

"Doesn't matter, these are my garden pants," she plopped down joyously and attacked cow parsley with vigor.

"I take it you like roses, and I suspect it was you who kept the bed in shape?" I said with sudden intuition. She flushed with shy defiance, nodding her head. "Thank you very much. Will you help me? You'll have to tell me what to do, but so many bushes—there'll be plenty of roses to share. Haven't you any roses in your garden?"

"With so many trees, there's never enough sun," she shook her head sadly. "They'd only die—so I worked on this one. The people didn't mind."

"I don't mind, either," I said warmly. "Let's make these the showiest bushes in town!"

Her small pointed face was illuminated by a grin, disclosing numerous gaps in the baby teeth. "Could we *try* to win a prize in the August Rose Show?" she breathed, ecstatically.

"Of course!"

I think she spent every blessed free second yearning over those roses! It seemed I never looked out a back window that I didn't see a small figure crouching on the grass verge, ruthlessly removing any weed so brazen as to raise its head—but roses were her only passion. She was politely uninterested in my nasturtiums, unenthusiastic over a dozen gladiola bulbs for the side bed, and actively displeased with the lush peony plants at the corner of the rose bed, shutting off light from the rosebush between them. The instant the peonies stopped blooming, she commanded they be cut down. "That rose can't *breathe!*" she said, ac-

cusingly. "I don't know why any one would put a
peony *there!*"

I didn't know why, either. I got the secateurs and
we massacred the peony at once.

Miss King nearly caught us the day we were absorbed in a new aphid spray, but fortunately, Pogo
yapped, and I looked up to find her bearing down on
us eagerly. "Oh dear," I said under my breath, dropping the can and scrambling to my feet. "Excuse
me . . ."

"Yeah, Miss Snoop," Suzanne agreed. "I think I'll
go too, Miss Robinson—back later."

Arthur had already gone; the tip of his black tail
was just disappearing behind the honeysuckle. I
pelted for the kitchen door, while Miss King called,
"Miss Robinson, Miss Robinson?" Briefly I paused and
called back, "Sorry—telephone," with a hypocritical
smile of regret . . . after which Arthur and I lurked in
the pantry until Suzanne tapped on the back door.

"She's gone. Let's finish before she gets back."

I felt an uneasy disloyalty to adults. "It's not that I
dislike Miss King," I said untruthfully, "but I haven't
time to talk to her today, you understand?"

"Yes. She just asks *questions*," Suzanne translated
calmly. "We don't like questions because of papa's
job."

"I see. Well, let's go." Fleetingly, I wondered if
papa was a T-man. I wasn't curious enough to ask,
and gradually a few things emerged. Mama was an
Italian teacher; papa did puzzles for the government,
and other puzzles at home for fun, but they were not
like my Double Crostics. They were groups of num-
bers or letters. "Cryptograms?" I suggested and she
nodded.

So Mr. Crosson was probably with a scientific group,
perhaps the moon shot. Who cared what he did? Although I couldn't imagine why he rented such a large
house, when his wife couldn't afford a cleaning wom-

an, but perhaps she enjoyed housework? Suzanne was
always impeccably clean, no matter how old and
faded the gardening clothes.

I wasted no time on the Crossons. I never saw him;
once when I was retrieving my newspaper from the
front steps, I faced an Italianate type unloading supermarket bags from an ancient blue Ford. We ex-
changed polite smiles. *Sic transit societas* . . . and I
was quite willing to keep it that way.

The days turned into weeks, and May became June.
I wrote Julian and Polly every Sunday, which was a
long established family habit; I had a letter from
them, sometimes long and sometimes short, every
Wednesday or Thursday. I had one letter from Sid
Abelson, reporting his luncheon with Anscot who
would admit only that "a member of the family" had
altered the instructions to the junior, who had been
too new to AVT to realize Anscot should have been
informed. Had I thought of anything more?

I wrote back that I was thinking of it as little as
possible, sorry—but of course "a member of the family" could only be Ludo himself. Who else could issue
instructions that would automatically be accepted by
a newcomer to AVT who knew only that the Trael account was *important*?

Aside from Miss King, nobody bothered me by for-
mal calls. The day she rang the bell, Peace Beloved
dealt with her firmly. "Miss Robinson ain't receiving
company," she stated, standing immovably in the
doorway. "She laid down on her bed, restin'."

"Has she been ill?" Miss King pounced. "What was
wrong? I had no idea, she never said she was con-
valescing . . ."

Peace Beloved might not be a giant intellect, but
she had imagination! "I don't rightly know," she confided, "but she still don't eat no more than a bird, and
she has to rest all day—*no company*. I'll tell her you

called, goodbye," and she shut the door in Miss King's face!

"You there, Miss Robinson?" She grinned up at me conspiratorially. "I got rid of her, you can come down now."

I couldn't resist a surreptitious peek at Miss King's figure retreating up the street—which was why I happened to see a man neatly parking a shiny red convertible before the Crossons' and walking up the front path. I caught my breath, shrank against the wall and clung to the telephone table for support. Almost I felt I might be going to faint.

Unless I was going out of my mind, the man was clearly, distinctly, recognizably—*George.*

He went casually up the steps and through the front door, as though he belonged there.

I'm only imagining, I told myself shakily—but if I weren't? I tottered blindly into the living room and sank into a chair. Dimly I could hear Peace Beloved singing, "Yeah-yeah-*yeah!*" over the ironing board in the basement. We'd agreed she might indulge in Beatles provided I were not within earshot.

The whole agonizing mess was right back with me. I knew now it'd never be finished until it was explained. These past weeks were only a semi-nirvana, a refusal to think, I might need a bromide pill at night, to cope with an empty bed, but in daylight it was more and more possible to forget Ludo's deep voice, wicked witty remarks *sotto voce* . . . he'd have had a field day with Miss King! I hadn't dared let myself think what he'd have said—and the rest of my new life was so totally estranged from that of Mrs. Ludovic Trael, I'd been able to submerge, to look from other, unfamiliar, windows of my mind.

If Mrs. Ludovic Trael wished roses, she telephoned Goldfarb or Constance Spry; if she desired *fillet de* .

boeuf roti, she sent word to the chef. Mrs. Ludovic Trael's bed was shared by Mr. Ludovic Trael—with no room for an Arthur, although candor compelled the admission that Arthur weighed far less. Mrs. Ludovic Trael would never have *dreamed* of instructing a Peace Beloved in the art of brioche in return for lessons in the subtleties of spoon bread—and if Mrs. Ludovic Trael had ever wished a fashionable hairdo, she would have gone to Kenneth, instead of chopping off her hair with the kitchen scissors and experimenting with a packet of milk bath Lilt.

Limply, I sat until I could summon strength to go out to the kitchen for a stiff highball. Evidently there is some *sort of plot, originating in that man.* I was still at sea for the *why.* I was certain I'd never seen him, never met him, yet if he could turn up here, he must be trailing me. *He* must know *me.* Could I possibly have met him at some college party—or among the young marrieds I'd known before I went to the Sorbonne? If *I* couldn't recall *him,* what could I have said or done to turn him into Nemesis?

Why was I so sure he was the man in the pictures? Was it only a chance resemblance of bone structure and hair *en brosse?* I knew it wasn't; my mind said flatly, *He's the man.* I'd recognized him instantly—but why? I forced myself to calmness, sipping the highball and thinking . . . Eventually I had it.

There was a small but distinct scar, tilting his right eyebrow askew with a most attractive deviltry. It had been clearly evident in even the quick glance I'd been permitted of the pictures. There was no doubt: *George* was next door.

Furthermore, he belonged there. He had a key.

Had he trailed me, or was it coincidence? Briefly, I was tempted to pack a bag and catch the next plane for somewhere, anywhere—but I couldn't spend my life running away from a total stranger! I still didn't know how or why the photographs were rigged. I was still certain Ludo was behind it. *Let's settle it once and for all.*

Once Peace Beloved had sashayed out the front door, I barred, bolted, locked, from top to bottom. *I will not be frightened,* I told myself, which was easier said than done, with Suzanne tapping at the kitchen door for an evening session with the roses. She was so insistent, I finally opened a crack. "Not tonight, sweetie. I'm dressing for a—dinner engagement."

"Okay," she said brightly, hopping off the back steps. "Have a good time."

"Ought you to be spending time over here tonight?" I asked artfully. "I thought you had company?"

"Company?" she looked puzzled. "You mean Uncle George? *He* isn't company," she said disdainfully, and hopped away in some private game toward the rose bed.

Uncle George?

I bolted the back door carefully, deliberately turned on the entrance carriage lanterns—as though merely gone for the evening. For two terrified hours I crouched on a cushion beside the dining room window, keeping my eyes on the house next door, while dusk deepened into night. Reason said if there were meant to be any sortie against me, it would occur after dark, when all latecomers straggling down the street from the Connecticut Avenue bus had reached home.

The Crossons were always thrifty with lights. Even now, there was only a dim electric candle in the living room. The kitchen and dining porch were lit, and the basement, which Peace Beloved said contained a bedroom and bath with a rec room and huge store closets. After a while the basement was dark, so they were probably at table . . . and finally, to my amazement, Uncle George emerged, going to the car with hand wavings and badinage I couldn't hear.

He slid behind the wheel and with a final wave,

roared away toward Connecticut Avenue. The porch
lights went off, and in the next hour I could chart
progress from clearing away (turn off dining room
lights), to wash dishes (darken the kitchen) to the
bedroom and upstairs study. Suzanne's room had been
briefly lit, then darkened, around nine, so she was
abed. The bedroom light went out at ten; the study
lamp was still on. Papa Crosson doing cryptograms for
fun?

I couldn't sit on the floor all night, and my tummy
was asking, *Is your throat cut?* I got up stiffly,
stretched the kinks out of my legs. In the kitchen, I
pulled down the window shade and used the refriger-
ator for light, leaving it open while I stuck frozen
shrimp curry into the oven and made a salad. While
the curry warmed, I felt my way to the living room
and set a heavy chair against each porch door. The
locks were squeaky, and I doubted anyone could open
them with a celluloid strip without arousing the neighborhood, but one never knows. Upstairs I found a
blanket and blacked out my bedroom window . . . after
which, I felt my way downstairs, set dinner on a tray,
and cautiously bore it back to the bedroom.

It was *hell*, and I was beginning to be more furious
than frightened. What did this man *want?* Was he
coming back, would he try to search this house as he'd
searched the hotel room? I was totally unprotected except for the fireplace poker which I'd remembered to
bring upstairs with me—and what use would it be
against a switchblade or gun?

Cautiously I reconnoitered from the master bedroom
window. There was no car, but of course it would be
parked out of sight. The house was completely dark;
papa had finished his puzzles and gone to bed, also.
Somehow I felt the heat was off, and for the first time
I wondered if it had ever been on . . . because George
must be extraordinarily confident, to arrive in broad

daylight and boldly enter by the front door? But perhaps it was part of the plan—that I should be un-
nerved by recognizing him?

There were still my front entrance lights.

I made ready for bed, and took the tray down to
the kitchen in my bare feet. I'd just set the thing on
the edge of the sink when there was a minor avalanche
from the coal bin: Arthur, mousing again. He'd never
caught but the one, but hope springs eternal with cats,
apparently, and whenever he had nothing better to
do, he was crawling over the nuggets and emerging,
mouseless, with filthy paws. I was already resigned to
having all Polly's rugs cleaned when I left . . . but on
top of my frightened evening, I jumped half out of
my skin at the noise.

Stalking over to the cellar steps, I flung open the
door and said, "*Arthur!* Will you *get* from there *at
once!*"

There was only silence—which brought my heart
to my throat, because Arthur always said "Mmmmwow?" in a particularly endearing tone when Spoken
To.

I stood rooted to the kitchen linoleum, staring into
darkness, knowing *someone* was down there. George?
Silently I backed away; there was no key in the door—
and I'd left the poker upstairs, of course. I would.
Could I make Julian's study phone to call the police?
Reason said there wouldn't be a key there, either. Run
to the front door—at this hour, who'd be abroad to
help me?

Listening intently, I could distinctly hear painfully
suppressed breathing, a tiny slither of motion, and I
was suddenly reckless. "I don't know who you are or
what you want, but I am calling the police," I said
with bravado and trampled boldly to the dining room
phone . . . only to hear a faint voice calling, "Hi! No,
Binks—don't!"

Ludo's voice? I whirled back to the steps and flipped the switch. For a second I thought it really was Ludo, lying spread-eagled at the bottom of the coal bin, until he said, "Sorry, Binks, it's me—Perryn," and between fright and disappointment, I was totally enraged. I stood at the top of the steps and swore at him in six languages until, surprisingly, he burst out laughing.

"It's not *funny*," I told him furiously. "Dammit, haven't you people done *enough* to make my life miserable, *what* are you doing down there? Your face is perfectly *filthy*, *will* you get to hell up here and explain yourself?"

"In a minute, if I can make it. I've wrenched my ankle."

"Crawl!" I suggested coldly, folding my arms and waiting.

Actually, that was more or less what he did, rolling to his knees with a grunt of pain and pulling himself up the steps, hand over hand on the railing, until he sank onto the kitchen stool, white-faced and exhausted. "*There's* a damn stupid thing," he complained bitterly. "A whacking great coal bin directly under the window. Who uses coal these days?"

"We own West Virginia," I said. "Explanation?"

He seemed not to hear. "What'n hell have you done to yourself?" he asked accusingly. "You're thin as a pikestaff, and you've *cut* your hair!"

"What's it to you? If you don't quit stalling, I shall still call the police," I assured him. "For the last time: *what are you doing here?* Playing jackal for your charming brother?"

Perryn's eyes blazed at me. "I might have expected that reaction," he said grimly. "By God, you certainly fooled us all. I have to hand it to you, Bi."

"Don't," I advised. "I'll only hand it right back, preferably between the eyes. How you have the consummate *gall* even to hold an opinion of me, let alone express it—after the filthy lies, the sweet framing job, darling Ludo pulled on me," I snarled, "and don't talk about who fooled whom! He hasn't even got the guts to come himself, sends his kid brother to do the job—whatever it is." I was working up for a good case of hysterics, I knew it; I didn't give a damn.

"So the Traels hang together? One for all, and all for one?" I spat. "I'd have thought your precious gang had done enough, but you're not through with me? Well, I'm through with you—all of you—and you can explain yourself to the police." I turned to the telephone, with Perryn protesting, "*No!* My God, Bi, think of the papers!"

"Yes, I'm thinking of them. They had a field day with me; I've nothing to lose. Let's see how the Traels will like it." I'd picked up the receiver when Perryn said, "Oh, all right . . .

"I want Ludo's notebooks."

I replaced the phone slowly, and looked at him in total bewilderment. "*I* don't have them; why on earth come to me?"

"Because you *did* have them," he said evenly. "Didn't you, Bi? You were using them for your history book or whatever it was."

"Yes, of course . . . but that was months and months ago."

Perryn nodded expressionlessly. "When did you realize what you'd got hold of, I wonder?" he remarked conversationally. "Well, the jig's up. I need those notebooks. It would save a major scandal if you'd hand them over peaceably."

"I tell you I don't have them," I said uncertainly. "Ludo knew I was finished; he must have taken them back—he was always borrowing one or another for a day or two, even while I was working. If you want the things, ask him."

"I can't," said Perryn in a strange undertone. "He's —gone."

I stared at him blankly. "You mean . . . *Ludo's dead?*" I whispered—and for the first time in my life, I fainted.

Chapter
5

I came to, lying full length on the dining room floor, with Perryn hobbling frantically about, drenching me with water and slapping my wrists. "My God, Bi—*no*, *he isn't dead* . . . d'you hear me? *He isn't dead!*"

"All right," I said feebly. "Will you *quit* throwing water; it's cold down here—and for heaven's sake, get *off* that ankle." On a level with his feet, I could see it disastrously puffed over the handsewn Italian moccasin.

"Never mind my ankle; can you get up?" he asked anxiously, still "pooring" my wrists.

I considered the question. Astonishingly, I discovered a total faint is rather restful. I was bodily limp, with an ache in my funnybone, but otherwise my mind was amazingly clear and clicking along like a Univac, producing total recall. Was Perryn my enemy? I thought not, but I was certain he held vital pieces of the puzzle. I closed my eyes briefly, *What's the use of a doctorate if you can't research a person as well as a book?*

I sat up with such suddenness, I *whanged* his head bending over me. "Ouch!" we chorused.

"Dammit, I'm sore from top to bottom," he complained, rubbing his forehead.

"Sorry," I apologized, scrambling awkwardly to my feet and looking at him thoughtfully. *What would be the best approach?* I decided on ingenuous frankness. "We're all at cross purposes," I said naïvely. "I *haven't* the notebooks—but why should you want them? Why did you have to try burglary, instead of simply ringing the front doorbell and asking me? Where is Ludo, anyway, and why did he send you here?"

"He didn't," Perryn said after a moment. "We'd better put our heads together."

"Oh, *definitely!* Where *is* Ludo?"

"*Quien sabe?*" he shrugged, struggling to his feet with a grunt. "Be easy; if he were dead, we'd know it," he said soberly.

"Well, what *do* you know?"

"He went straight from the courthouse to the boat— and that's the last anyone's seen or heard of him," Perryn said baldly.

"No radiophone to the office?" I could feel my heart pounding again when he shook his head, because it added up to a hundred, in my mind. The divorce wasn't final for three months; Ludo was pre-honeymooning on the boat, and naturally keeping out of communication. One whisper that he'd jumped the gun, and the decree would be denied.

There was still *why*, with which Perryn might help. "Can you get to the living room?" I slid a shoulder under his arm for support, and he limped to the couch while I turned on a light. "Take off shoe and sock; I'll get something."

When I came back with witch hazel and an old napkin, he gritted his teeth while I felt about gently, cudgelling my wits for the first aid course, but fortunately it wasn't broken. "Only a nasty sprain," I said consolingly, soaking the bandage and positioning the ottoman. "Keep it up!"

Perryn nodded faintly, his eyes still closed, and I had a sudden suspicion. "When did you last eat?" He twisted against the couch cushions impatiently.

"I don't know—lunchtime, I think."

"Lie still while I get something." Perryn was far too much *man* to go twelve hours without food. I brought

him a stiff drink, set cigarettes and lighter to hand.
"Ten minutes . . ." He merely nodded again, silently,
and I went back to scramble eggs, slice the biggest
tomato, butter hot toast and heat the breakfast coffee.
I set the tray on the coffee table. "Eat first, talk later—
and keep the foot up!"

He was ravenous; in another ten minutes he'd
cleaned up every crumb, was wiping his mouth with a
sigh. "Good Lord, you can cook?"

"Yes," I said flatly. "*Now:* why did you think I had
the notebooks—and why do you want them?"

Replete with warm food, he was less tractable. I
realized dismally, *it was a mistake to feed him before
I picked his brains* . . . but would I know? This was
my first experience of cloak-and-dagger. He took his
time lighting a cigarette and sipping coffee, until I
said, "You've had enough time to figure the gen, Let's
have it."

"I thought you had the books because you were using them," he said carefully, "and I want them for a
clue to where Ludo's gone. Sufficient?"

I shook my head. "I can tell you where he's gone—
or more or less," I said calmly, "but I'm not about to
until I have the truth," as he looked up eagerly.

"That is the truth," he said warily, "and for God's
sake, Bi—if you know or suspect anything, tell me."

"It isn't *all* the truth, is it?" I'd had time in the
kitchen, to get used to the idea of Ludo . . . honey-
mooning. I still meant to know whatever Perryn knew.
"*Why* is it important for you to trace Ludo?" I mused
reflectively. "He was always disappearing into the wild
blue yonder; he always turned up safe and sound, even
when out of touch for a while. Why the flap *now*, I
wonder?

"And why attempted burglary?" I went on steadily.
"Even if I had the books, why should you think I'd refuse to give them to you—or if there was protocol
about asking me directly, why not your lawyers asking

mine?" I picked up the tray. "When I have every single thing you know—then I'll tell you what I think."

In the kitchen I deliberately fixed another tray with glasses and the brandy bottle, not that it would do more than demonstrate good will. Even Rafe, who could develop wobbly legs, was never foxed—while Ludo and Perryn could have set the whole Russian Army under the table drinking nothing but vodka on an empty stomach!

Arthur had deserted to the enemy, I discovered as I set down the tray. He was stretched blissfully the length of Perryn's chest, purring raucously beneath expert tickling. Perryn smiled at me lazily. "Who's your familiar?"

"That's Arthur—because he spends nights on the round table," I filled brandy glasses. "At least he did in his former home," as Perryn chuckled and extended a long arm for his *fine*. "His people went to South Africa, and I don't have a round table, so he sleeps on my feet."

"Lucky beast!" Perryn commented, eyeing me over the liqueur glass, while I lit a cigarette and ignored the flattery.

"Well?" I said after a moment.

"Yes—the answers," he agreed soberly, still looking at me. "I can't believe . . ." he muttered involuntarily, and pressed his lips together, studying the brandy glass. "All right. They said definitely not, but I've already loused everything up by getting caught—and Ludo's more important to me."

"*They?*"

His eyes were impersonal. "The FBI."

Of all things I might have expected, that was the *last;* I said so. "How the hell do *they* come into my divorce? Good God, with all the Commies and Nazis and Ku Kluxers running about making trouble, don't tell me J. Edgar has time for *my* supposed peccadilloes?" I caught my breath. "Or—is Ludo in trouble over those photographs?" I asked tensely.

"How could he be in trouble?" Perryn asked, puzzled.

"Don't you know they were rigged? Don't you know—*he* had them made, himself, in order to get rid of me finally and forever?" I whispered. "Don't you know that's where he is, right this minute: *on the boat with your next sister-in-law*, hiding out until the decree is final?"

Perryn sat up with a bounce, dislodging Arthur ruthlessly. "No," he said flatly. "I don't know it and I don't believe a word of it. You must be out of your mind, Bi!"

"Oh, I can't combat the Trael solidarity," I shrugged cynically, "but I can still put two and two together."

"Coming out with three and a half," he said bitingly, "except you got caught in the middle. So *that's* your game: throw everything onto Ludo?" His face darkened with fury. "By God, he was right; he always called you a clever puss. Well, I'm damned if I'll let you blacken one of the best brains in the country just because you want to have your cake and eat it too—with plenty of money *and* a younger man."

"Is *that* what Ludo wants everyone to think?" I said slowly. "But—why?"

"It's not what he *wants*, but what's the truth," he snorted harshly. "Isn't it, Bi? Isn't it true you transcribed every word of his coded diaries and gave it to your lover for sale to the highest bidder? Hah! Well, *George* isn't a smart cookie like you; he sold too soon, didn't he? He rocked the boat, and Ludo found out." He pulled himself up and towered over her, bracing himself on the carved wooden arm of the couch.

"D'you know, even when they'd traced the whole thing, even when he had to admit *you* were the only other person in the world who could have deciphered them, Ludo wouldn't believe it for *three months?* He fought the whole United States Government for you, Bianca—until those pictures turned up. Then he *knew*," Perryn said grimly. "Rafe told me how he took it. Ludo's a Trael; even for his wife, he wouldn't condone treason—but you broke his heart, damn you . . . *damn you!*"

Looking at Perryn's near-murderous eyes and contemptuous expression, I smelt truth—but as Sid had said, it was only what Perryn *believed* to be truth. I knew it wasn't. "Sit down," I said authoritatively. He hesitated, still glaring at me. "Most of this I never heard before," I told him quietly, "but we are going to get to the bottom of it right now. *Sit down!*"

Slowly, he sank back on the couch, while I stood up. "As God is my witness," I said evenly, "*I* have truly believed *Ludo* rigged the pictures, *Ludo* framed me to get an immediate clear divorce, in order to marry another woman. Talk about broken hearts?" I smiled. "How d'you think I felt—when all he ever needed was to *ask* for freedom?" Perryn's eyes flickered, uncertainly.

"Now you turn up with an accusation of treason," I went on, "and that's a bit much. Oh, I'm sure you believe it—but I tell you right now: I'll take courtroom slime, but not even the great Ludovic Trael will brand *me* a traitor for his own ends. No," as Perryn opened his mouth, "my ancestors fought to make this country, too, and *I* have rights. I shall now make a fresh pot of coffee, after which we will thrash this out—*or I will call the FBI.* Is that clear?"

He nodded sulkily and relapsed on the couch. Arthur accompanied me to the kitchen, which was obscurely comforting, as apparently he did not wish food but merely wreathed around my ankles lovingly as I leaned against the counter and tried to pull my mind into usable order.

Ludo's notebooks?

They were a series of black, limp, leatherbound diaries, in which Ludo kept a daily log of his trips. They began ten or fifteen years back, when he'd first started minor chores for our Government, and they were in a personal code he'd developed purely for the sake of saving time and space. There were notes on ancient quarries and mines, descriptions of the countryside, together with all sorts of local lore Ludo found of interest. It was that stuff he'd offered me for expanding my thesis to *First Clues*.

Then a magazine asked for something on Arabia, if I had it? Ludo hunted out two enchanting fairy tales, and somehow the diaries were left permanently in my study, standing between bookends that were Siamese cats carved of chrysoprase. The current volume was always with him on the boat, and it was true, every now and then Ludo'd take one to refresh his memory for an upcoming trip. I never worried if one was missing; they were in his code and who else would want them?

Even in code, Ludo wrote vividly, and there were delightful legends and folklore, unused for the book. Skipping over the technical stuff, I'd extracted that material more for my own amusement than with a plan—only to find I had a new book. I hadn't told anyone, not even Helen, because I hadn't known myself until I'd finished and realized how much manuscript I had.

The publisher of *First Clues* had done well enough out of it to be *delighted* with a follow-up. He bought it in twenty-four hours; it was dedicated to Ludo, to be issued on his birthday, August 1st—and the first copy off the press was being bound to match his personal copy of *First Clues*.

Waiting for the water to seep through the Chemex filter, I pondered. There probably was an immense amount of useful information in those books for a min-

ing engineer. I wasn't—but my brother was a noted
petroleum geologist! *Do they think it's Julian?* I wondered frantically, and raced into the living room.

"Julian has *nothing* to do with this," I said loudly.
"He's been out of the country for five years, he only
came to help me. You're not to involve him in this, or
I will *really* break this thing wide open, if I have to
hire time on television!"

Perryn blinked at me dazedly, evidently half asleep
"Julian?" he inquired. "My God, how many men do
you have, Bi? First you're yelling for 'Arthur'—and
there's 'George' in the pictures—and you're protecting
someone called Julian?"

"Don't be silly," I said patiently. "You know Arthur's
the cat—and Julian's my brother who owns this house
—and George turns out to be next door, which was
why I was going to call the police, because I thought
you were he in the cellar."

Perryn came awake and sat up like a jack in the
box. "*George* is next door?" he said suspiciously. "I
thought you said you didn't know him?"

"I don't," I said shakily, "and I was scared to death
when I saw him. Oh, nothing makes sense!" I went for
the coffee and returned to find him sitting up, keen-
eyed and alert. He lit two cigarettes and thrust one at
me as I sat down.

"Tell!" he directed.

I told—ending with the search after Julian had
gone. "I thought it was someone sent to retrieve my
emerald engagement ring—and don't fly into high
stirrups, Perryn! After what I'd been through, the
courtroom smear, the furs and jewels cleaned out, do
you admit? That ring is valuable and Ludo could
never get it back legally."

Slowly his faced relaxed, and he nodded.

"But I knew almost at once it wasn't the ring," I
went on, "because I was asleep on the coach. Anyone
could have knocked me out and taken it—and an or-

dinary hotel thief would have taken my private jewelry even if it weren't particularly valuable, you see? Until you turned up tonight, I hadn't a clue as to what was wanted; I just made tracks!"

"That explains a lot," Perryn murmured sardonically. "Evidently you slipped your tail in the process, creating instant consternation—and while they were mobilizing to pick you up, they took their eyes off Ludo," he chuckled, "who promptly weighed anchor and ho! for the bounding main." He laughed heartily. "All right, go on."

"Well, they must have known I wasn't trying to dodge anyone," I objected. "I went to LaGuardia, signed the boarding pass with my own name, openly had a drink at the bar . . ."

"Oh, I'm sure they'd found you before you got to Washington," he agreed, "and *I* would think your openness ought to have made them think, too—but of course they were positive they had a case."

"I've been here ever since," I shrugged. "I've been nowhere but to shop, and put my rings in a deposit box," I inserted with delicate emphasis. "I've seen no one, had no visitors. I haven't much acquaintance in Washington, and I wasn't in a mood to call the few people I know. I've written only to my brother: the only mail is his letters to me, and one from my lawyer."

"What are you using for money?" he asked. "The bank admitted there were no withdrawals; you hadn't visited the box. Do admit, yourself: it looked like a planned flitting!"

"Julian gave me a check to go on with. I wasn't sure Ludo hadn't somehow blocked my checking account along with everything else and I'm not anxious for a bouncing check," I said evenly. "I meant to phone Abelson to inquire discreetly. It would have to be a bank transfer, anyway. I'm Miss Robinson down here; I don't want any connection with Bianca Trael."

"That's a filthy thing to say," he protested angrily, "as if Ludo *would!*"

"Why not? He did everything else—and now you tell me he's set the FBI on my tracks. I can scarcely be blamed for the teentsiest quiver of a doubt, surely?"

"They were onto you long before Ludo was," he countered grimly, "and you're not out of it yet."

"No, so I realize," I agreed. "Out of the blue within a few hours, I finally *see* this man I've never seen before in my life, who turns out to be the uncle of the child next door who works on my rose garden—and simultaneously, the younger brother of the man who's dragged me through a divorce court is found breaking and entering—looking for something I haven't got and accusing me of treason!

"So *you* will now explain—because unless you convince me this is not a put-up game from Ludo, it will be not you, *but I* who calls the FBI."

"I'm beginning to think we should call 'em anyway," he muttered, pounding fist into palm worriedly. "They wouldn't give me more than the time of day, I had to follow a hunch, make my own conclusions. They wouldn't help an inch, beyond agreeing to alert Interpol."

I glanced at the clock, which said two A.M. "Too late. You talk. Then we decide whether to phone. How did you know I was here?"

"Anscot said your brother was in court, it figured you'd hide out in his home," Perryn shrugged. "The address was in one of the scientific *Who's Whos*. He's rather a big gun, isn't he?" he commented.

"Yes," I said calmly, "he's a very big gun indeed, and it was kind of him to back me up. So you came down on the chance?"

Perryn nodded. "I drove around for a while, I saw you in the garden," he said. "I waited until it was dark, parked the car and walked back. It looked as though you were out for the evening. The car was there, but I supposed your date had picked you up. I couldn't see any sign of life, so after a while I made a try for it." He snorted slightly. "I should have known that window was booby-trapped; all too easy— slip the hand through, release the bolts, swing it back . . . next thing I knew, I was skidding tail over teacup with nothing to grab, ending slambang on my ankle— and *you*, standing up there yelling '*Arthur*', when all along I'd understood the guy was *George!*"

He grinned ruefully. "Obviously I was never meant to be a cat burglar. Ludo's bigger than I—and he moves like a butterfly."

I suppressed the instant memory of that silent, panther-footed, Indian-file walk—a man who could handle height and bulk with grace in a rare china shop, whose hands could lift a woman into his arms without effort—yet hold a fragile crystal goblet in delicate fingers. "Why didn't you ring the bell?"

He leaned forward, concentrating, and then spoke rapidly. "I was abroad. All I had was a letter from Rafe saying you'd turned up bitch, and Ludo was beside himself because it was worse than adultery; disregard newspapers; Ludo had to make a definite case, but was trying to keep it within bounds for your sake—not that you deserved it. I'm only telling you what I was told," he said to my involuntary protest.

"I suppose so. Go on," I forced myself to calmness.

"I wasn't needed; it was over; I went directly to New Mexico. I did think it odd I heard nothing from Ludo," he said slowly, "but I was busy with new stock and pasturage. I spoke to Rafe once; he only said Ludo was away."

"But why didn't he say they hadn't heard from him?"

He shrugged. "You know Rafe."

"No," I said flatly, "I don't know any of you, and don't huff and puff," as he snorted angrily. "I've had

plenty of time to realize I'm no smarter than a grun-
ion, but it doesn't make me any happier. So I *don't*
know Rafe. Explain him."

"Oh, well—I suppose it's compensation for being
middling," Perryn muttered. "He isn't the Head, and
he isn't the Benjamin, either; he hates being a De-
Courcy instead of a six-foot Trael. He admires Ludo
more than anyone on earth, and for six years he was
first. Then I turned up, and I was a Trael, d'you see?
Mother died when I was ten, and that left Rafe odd
man out in more ways than one. He not only didn't
look like us; he was away at college, while Ludo was
finished and home—and we were getting to be friends.

"It seemed I'd replaced Rafe with Ludo," Perryn
said simply. "He *really* knows he isn't left out, but unconsciously he's forever trying to assert himself, convince everyone he still comes *first.* He can't admit he
isn't in the know, not fully in Ludo's confidence before
anyone else. We go along with it. Ludo lets him make
a show of running the business, and he always sent a
message to Rafe when he talked to David Corey.

"So first, Rafe thought David was lying, that he
was in touch but wouldn't tell, and for some reason
Ludo was ignoring him . . . which was the very last
thing he'd admit until forced to it. Actually, David
was about to call me on his own. He'd worked up to
trying for contact every hour on the hour round the
clock for three days, with no reply."

I gulped. "He might be dead, the ship might have
foundered?"

Perryn shook his head firmly. "Quit the fantasies,"
he said with rough kindliness, "and use your head. If
he were dead, no matter what his instructions, nothing
would prevent Captain Holt from alerting us at once.
If the ship were in trouble, we'd have heard by now."

"I suppose," I said tremulously. "Rafe finally let
you know—why?"

"Binks, sweetie!" He protested sardonically. "You

have heard of the trust?" At my nod, "On May 15th annually, the head of the family approves stock changes, signs paper, distributes income. Failing personal appearance of Ludo, *that's the day the money stops.* I can manage without. The ranch is mine, it's in the black. So I wouldn't play baccarat in Monaco," he shrugged, "I could still ski at Sun Valley or spend a week in Vegas—but as of May 16th, *any* year, Rafe will be in grave financial difficulties.

"Apparently he pushed along with his salary check for walking-around money for a few weeks, hoping Ludo'd show. When he didn't, Rafe panicked and sent for me."

There was a long silence while I pondered his words. Perryn looked at me curiously. "D'you really not know Rafe and Helen are always on the thin edge of nothing?" he asked finally. "Ludo had to buy the apartment you found for them—not but what he thought it a good investment in order to get rid of them. I must say, I always wondered how they managed to furnish so magnificently."

"Me," I said after a moment, in a very small voice.

"You?" he echoed, genuinely startled.

I nodded. "Helen had never had a home of her own, she'd always had to live with other people's things, and *I* even pushed her out of those. It didn't seem fair, somehow—and I never spent *half* my allowance." Beneath his keen eyes, I felt troubled. "She said there wasn't money to furnish after Rafe bought the apartment," I faltered.

He looked at me impassively. "How—*interesting*," he drawled, thoughtfully. "You can prove it, of course?"

"Prove it?" I stared at him. "Why—ask Helen!"

"Did Ludo know you paid for Helen's furnishings?"

I shook my head. "It was just an arrangement between Helen and myself, but Rafe must have known."

"Not necessarily," Perryn said slowly. "He may have

thought she managed it on her gambling. She played high, and she always had better luck than he . . ."

"I never knew she gambled . . ."

"She wouldn't be likely to tell you, my sweet," he remarked drily, "particularly when she was conning you into paying for everything. How much did it run you: seventy-five grand?"

"Nearer eighty," I admitted, anxiously, "but I didn't need it, Perryn, and it was all in the family, after all."

His eyes flickered oddly. "You know we share the trust equally?" I nodded, uncomprehending. "Did it *never* occur to you," he commented, "that if Ludo could maintain fully staffed houses in New York and Paris, plus a sea-going yacht, plus a wife in emeralds and ermine draped over *carte blanche* from Balenciaga, *Rafe* should be able to do the same?

"Particularly after living rent-free for a dozen years in Ludo's house?" he said. I shook my head uncertainly. "You knew Rafe drew a salary for turning up at the office occasionally, didn't you? And since I don't have a wife, I could afford to buy a ranch to equal the Kings—plus building a hundred-thousand-dollar house, with every possible extra including a private plane? And Ludo's a dollar-a-year man for the Government. If anything, Rafe and I ought to have *more* money than he does! I

"So why—on an annual income of five hundred thousand dollars—should my brother's wife require your assistance for her furnishings, Bi?" he finished softly. "Are you *sure* that's where the money went?"

"Of course I'm sure," I said absently, occupied in considering his words. "I told you: ask Helen."

"I shall."

I only half heard him, trying to make sense out of this. "I never knew it was so *much*," I said suddenly. "I knew there was plenty, of course, but all Ludo ever said was how he liked things, and all I did was manage it. The bills went to the office; my allowance was

credited to my account; Miss English balanced the
books once a month. If I needed cash, someone got
it for me from the bank."

I looked at Perryn helplessly. "I suppose I'm pretty
stupid; Julian says I am," I told him with what dignity I could muster, "but I never exactly *looked* at my
checkbook. Mostly I used it for donations, when they
wanted Mrs. Ludovic Trael for a patroness. Then I'd
see how much the traffic would bear, depending on
how far to allowance day. I always kept enough so I
wouldn't run out if I had to make another donation,
but otherwise the money just piled up. That's why I
had enough for Helen."

"Did Ludo know that was how you worked your
account?"

"I don't know what he knew. I told you, we never
talked about money. It was Helen who told me about
the trust—but not how much." I sat silent, my fingers
plucking nervously at the housecoat skirts. "I don't
understand why Rafe let her think he'd paid for the
apartment."

"How d'you know he did? And don't *you* huff and
puff," Perryn said evenly. "I know Nell better than
you do . . . although I'm bound to say Ludo's always
too close-mouthed for comfort." He rumpled his hair
violently. "Well, anyway—Rafe sent for me, and he
was worried about money but I was worried about
Ludo, because it isn't like him to disappear. Even if
you're right about another woman, that wouldn't prevent his talking to David Corey. Who's to know what
passengers are aboard?"

"Yes," I agreed, "a boat is *much* better than a *mai-
son de rendezvous.*"

Perryn's lips tightened, but he ignored my comment. "When David was worried, I knew it was the
McCoy, and I asked questions until finally Rafe told
me . . ."

"*What?*"

"That a vital piece of information on mining conditions in Africa had leaked, creating a near-incident for our Government," he said evenly, holding my eyes steadily. "There is no slightest doubt the information originated in Ludo's diaries—and aside from Ludo, *you are the only other person in the world who can decipher his code.*

"Well," I said after a moment, "there's at least *one* other person—because I never transcribed anything for anybody, Perryn, and it wouldn't be Ludo himself."

"It wouldn't?"

"Oh, don't be *silly*," I said crossly, thinking backward. "*Anyone* could have taken those books, you know; they were just left in my study."

"But *not* anyone could read them. Ludo told the FBI to find another explanation. Apparently they didn't think there was another, and eventually they made a case."

I stared at him, open-mouthed. "In heaven's name, *how?*"

"By a large unexplained deposit to your account the previous week, plus equally large unexplained withdrawals running back several years. Rafe knew something was bothering Ludo. About a week before the balloon went up, Ludo admitted there'd been a leak and the FBI was working on it.

"Then, that morning, he and Rafe met, walking to the office. The FBI men waltzed in exactly as Ludo reached the reception room, with transcripts of your bank statements; half an hour later the pictures were delivered. Some of this I pried out of Judy at the reception desk, some from Miss English, some in guesswork," Perryn inserted, "and from your version, there's still more to it. But you do see how neatly it fitted, Bi?

"The FBI isn't used to innocent explanations; they suggested you were being blackmailed, had sold the information to pay off without Ludo's knowledge, and the pictures clinched the argument. You know Ludo's temper?" Perryn observed impersonally. "David was there to take notes. He says Ludo took one look at the pictures and went berserk; everybody in the office could hear him."

I was sitting on the edge of the ottoman, now, clenching my hands and feeling tears spilling, running down my cheeks. It was all so much worse than I'd dreamed—and still, in a way better, because now I knew what had happened, it could be cleared up. "Go on, please."

"They sent Miss English for your cancelled checks, and the big ones—the very ones they questioned— were all drawn simply to cash, Binks. That's why I asked if you could prove you gave the money to Helen," Perryn said. "Rafe says what killed Ludo was your disloyalty, plus that deposit. He couldn't get over that; he kept saying 'if she needed more money for anything, anything at all including blackmail, she had only to ask'."

"I didn't need money," I finally found my voice. "That was money I *earned*, for another book! It was a surprise, for Ludo's Birthday. It *was* unused material from his diaries, yes, but only the legends. Nobody knew, because it was only fill-in work," I explained earnestly. "When I had nothing else to do. I thought it was a pity nobody could read them because of Ludo's code. I thought I'd just transcribe for the rest of you, and perhaps have a dozen copies privately printed— but there were so many, it turned into a book.

"Oh, I was so proud of it," I wailed. "It's a book club selection for August; the first copy is being bound to match *First Clues*." I fumbled for Kleenex and mopped my eyes dismally.

"Well, well," Perryn murmured, narrowing his eyes. "This is definitely a horse of another color."

"Why didn't he ask me?" I cried, furiously. "Don't

you see why I think he did it all himself, Perryn? I wasn't asked to explain any of these things: I wasn't let to say a word for myself . . . because he knew there'd *be* an explanation to ruin the beautiful case he'd built up!

"He won't thank you for coming down and spilling the beans," I said sarcastically. "That's his only slip: not letting you hear from him until you were worried. If *I'd* disappeared, it would probably suit him down to the ground."

Surprisingly, Perryn leaned forward with a laugh and pulled me bodily from the ottoman into his arms on the couch. "My sweet chucklehead," he said affectionately, "now it's *you* who's being silly! Why d'you think Ludo was so violent over all this! Because he's *crazily* in love with you—and he never could control himself over a disappointment in people." With one arm he cuddled me against his shoulder, while he blotted up the tears with his handkerchief, talking calmly all the while.

"You made me explain Rafe to you? Maybe I should explain Ludo, too," he said soberly. "He never even *thought* he ever loved another woman in his life; he never expected to marry, even to carry on the name. It was always agreed that was up to me, since Rafe didn't seem to be getting anything out of Helen.

"When it turned out dangerous for you, he put it right back in my lap," Perryn smiled ruefully, "and frankly, I wasn't so keen any more—after seeing the two of you together. You haven't a sister, by any chance?"

"You know I haven't," I sniffled. "Please, don't talk about Ludo."

"All right, I won't—except to say I know my brother better than you do," he said gently. "He's brilliant, and world-famous, and when he fell in love, he couldn't believe it was true. After twenty years of women throwing themselves at him all over the world, threatening to kill themselves for him, willing to risk any scandal to be with him," Perryn's voice was soft, "Ludo couldn't *believe* a beautiful virgin could love an international rake who was fifteen years her senior.

"I don't know who's done what," he said grimly, "but I'll swear he's as much in the dark as you are."

"Then where *is* he?" I sobbed distractedly.

"Shhh, he's on the boat somewhere, wrestling with himself," Perryn patted my shoulder absently. "Enough tears," he said suddenly, pushing me upright and sitting up behind me. "Now we're going to have to think, which requires clear heads. Bed! Tomorrow we'll put it together."

It was only after lights out, as I was falling asleep, that I thought of Miss King . . . and Julian's admonitions over staid conduct . . . as well as Peace Beloved, who was giving me Saturday in order to cope with spiders in the cellar and moths in the closets.

I bounced out of bed, threw on a robe and paddled across to the master bedroom to shake Perryn's shoulder ruthlessly. "Wha'?" he inquired sleepily.

"You have to be a family cousin," I hissed. "D'you hear me? You're *a cousin!*"

" 'M a cousin," he muttered agreeably, opening one eye. "Why don't you have a sister?" he yawned gigantically.

"Because I was a menopause baby and the end of the line," I said, impatiently, "and you'll be the end of the line if you don't remember your name is Mr. Perryn . . ." His eyelids were already closed, and in sleep he was too like Ludo for comfort. I turned off the light and went back to my bed, where Arthur waited politely until I'd arranged myself, after which he draped himself comfortably across my toes.

My last conscious thought was, "Lawkamussy me, can this be *I?*"

Chapter
6

Perryn was apparently still sleeping exhaustedly when Peace Beloved arrived, accompanied by Beatles, about ten A.M. I could hear her six houses away, and my first thought was to glance to the curb next door, but it was bare of shiny red cars. I sighed with relief, although I was no longer quite so alarmed. Whether or not Perryn believed me or was playing a deep game, I felt certain he'd protect me physically.

My maid now appeared beneath the trees shading the sidewalk, prancing along and singing, "Yeah-yeah-*yeah!*" She turned up the front path, but was unable to tear herself from Beatles until the last possible moment. Evidently she'd set the transistor on the mail box while she hunted for the key, and crashed open the front door with her usual joyous abandon, sending a wave of Beatles soaring through the house.

"*Will* you *stop* that filthy racket?" Perryn bellowed, bursting irascibly from his bedroom and producing instant silence from Peace Beloved.

She stepped delicately into the hall, closed the front door like a mouse, and called anxiously, "Miss Robinson, you got a *cold?*"

"No," I said suppressing laughter, while Perryn glared at me and stalked back to his bed. "It's all right, Peace Beloved. I'll be right down."

She was still mouselike when I reached the kitchen. "That was our cousin, Mr. Perryn," I explained. "He arrived unexpectedly, and he's very tired, so I think we'll start in the cellar and do the closets when he's waked up."

"A gentleman visitor?" Peace Beloved's eyes sparkled with anticipation. "Hot cakes, sausages, eggs and toast?" she inquired hopefully. Breakfast was the best thing she did, and my limited menu a constant regret.

"He'll eat all of that and then some," I assured her, realizing I'd have to market again, to cover the weekend.

"How long he going to stay?"

That was a good question, I thought. What was he doing here in the first place? There was a piece of paper somewhere in a New York court that said officially Perryn and I were no longer related . . . and neither of us had remembered it for a minute last night. We'd snapped at each other, been at cross purposes—and we were still brother and sister by marriage, sliding back into familial friendliness. By all the rules of decorum I should have sent him to a hotel. It had never occurred to either of us.

But the instant he poked his nose outside, Miss King would spot him, and even billed as a cousin, Perryn was far too young and handsome not to create *gossip*. He wouldn't be able to drive with that ankle for a day or so, either. "I don't know just how long he'll stay . . . a day of two," I said evasively. "Come on."

We went down cellar and attacked spiders with the vacuum-cleaner brush. I found the task unnerving, but apparently spiders ranked next to Beatles in Peace Beloved's estimation, and she pursued them with cries of satisfaction. "Oh, no, you don't gets away!" she said, whopping the brush on arachnids hastening in every direction. "Hi-yi, I got you!" Eventually I left her to organized murder and went up for another cup of coffee. I could hear movements above. "Perryn?"

"Yes," he leaned over the landing rail, harassed. "Where's the shower?"

"There isn't one."

"How do I get *clean?*"

"Take a bath." I went up to find the biggest bath-sheet, while he stared at himself disgustedly in the bathroom mirror.

"I suppose there isn't a razor?"

"Only a ladies, electric." I found it and left him staring at it dubiously. "Yell when you're getting dressed, so Peace Beloved can get your breakfast ready."

"Peace Beloved?" he repeated blankly. "My God, Bi, where d'you get these people?"

"They're part of the new me," I told him calmly, and returned to my tepid coffee. Looking absently from the kitchen window, I saw Suzanne communing with the roses. She was not in gardening pants, but attired in a *good* dress. She inspected each bush critically and finally came to the back door.

"Good morning," but Suzanne ignored the amenities.

"We're going to Rehoboth for the weekend, and the roses have to be watered *tonight*," she said, eyeing me with definite distrust. "I won't be here, will you?"

"Yes," I felt my heartbeat quickening. "When will you be back?"

"Tomorrow night, but late, so you might have to water again," she said.

"I'll take care of everything. Have a good time."

She kicked her toe against the bottom step, faintly sulky. "I won't, I hate the beach," she muttered. "Nothing but hot dogs and sand."

"Oh well, it's only overnight," I said bracingly, "and I'll water. What about dusting?"

"It can wait till Monday. I'd rather do it myself, if you don't mind. Well—goodbye, Miss Robinson . . ."

"Goodbye . . ." On a hunch I reconnoitered from the dining room window—to see a shiny red convertible turning the corner. Frantically I flew up the stairs to pound on the bathroom door. "Perryn—he's here again, *quick!* Come see if *you* recognize him!"

"Who's here?"

"*George!*" I shrieked at him, exasperated. "Come *on!*"

I flew to the corner window, as Perryn plunged out of the bathroom in his underpants, the razor still in his hand, and peered over my shoulder. "Get the license number," he said intently, "although I bet it's a Hertz rental. Maryland DH-4632." I found paper and pencil in the study, hastily jotted the number, and came back.

George was leisurely climbing out, coming up the front walk next door. He was wearing slacks and sports coat, and in the clear morning light he was more natty than elegant, although attractive if you liked the type. As if by telepathy, he glanced directly toward our window. Instinctively I shrank aside, but Perryn peered intently through the crack of the blind.

"I never saw him before," he muttered. "What makes you so sure, Bi? He looks totally ordinary, like any dozen chaps you'd find all over town. If you don't know him, how can you be so positive?"

"The *scar* over his eye!" I hissed wildly. "If you'd seen those pictures . . ."

"I did," he said, dropping the blind as the man vanished onto the porch, "and I don't remember a scar—but if you're right . . ." He stood thoughtfully for a moment, turned back to the bathroom. "Down in ten minutes," he said, and closed the door behind him.

I alerted Peace Beloved. Then I hovered in the dining room, pretending to set the table and keeping an eye on the red car . . . and in a few minutes there was a procession. George, carrying a couple of valises, mama burdened with wicker baskets of picnic food, Suzanne clutching a revolting rubber floating elephant complete with trunk that obscured papa, as he bent to double-lock the front door. Then they were all going away from me, climbing into the car, and as Perryn came downstairs, they drove away.

"They've gone," I said tremulously.

"Good," he said casually, throwing a long arm about me and planting a kiss on my temple. "Good morning, *cousin!*" he remarked with a grin. "Stop shaking and sit down. And *you*," he observed flatteringly as she bustled in with coffee pot and orange juice, "are Peace Beloved. How do you do?"

Peace Beloved stopped short, ran her eyes slowly from toes to top of Perryn and popped her gum explosively. "Whoo-*ooo*, you a powerful lot o' man, Mr. Perryn," she said, awed. "I better beat up another batch of cakes . . ."

"Does she always make that noise?" he asked dazedly, drawing up to the table.

"Oh no, bubble gum and Beatles are proscribed," I said calmly, "but under stress of emotion, she forgets herself—and you *are* a powerful lot of man, after all."

He tossed off the orange juice, bottoms up, and set down the glass as Peace Beloved trotted in with what appeared to be six scrambled eggs flanked by a dozen sausages, plus four slices of hot buttered toast. Silently, he cleaned the plate. "Your scrambled eggs were better," he murmured absently.

"Her hot cakes are better," I assured him—and on cue, Peace Beloved whisked in with the first stack, slipping aside the empty plate with a chuckle of satisfaction and planking the cakes proudly before him. "One more stack going to hold you, Mr. Perryn—or could you eat another?" she inquired hopefully.

"One will be enough, thanks," he said indistinctly. "Whoo-*ooo*, Peace Beloved, you are a powerful lot of cook!" he added flatteringly. She giggled shyly and popped the gum again from excitement.

"How long you going to stay, Mr. Perryn?" she

asked, while he recoiled slightly. "You'd like for me to make some light rolls? And I could easy as not come out tomorrow to get your breakfast."

"How long am I going to stay," he echoed looking at me thoughtfully. "Why, I'm a fixture for the time being, and if you guarantee hot cakes like these, you'd better come every day, Peace Beloved," he said cheerfully.

"Now, wait a minute, she has other clients," I began, but Peace Beloved wasn't minded to lose her chance for glory.

"Shoo, Miss Robinson, my sister-in-law can take 'em—or they can go dirty one week," she said nonchalantly. "I be here tomorrow, Mr. Perryn. What time you like breakfast on Sunday?"

He waggled his eyebrows at me wickedly. "Eleven?"

"Yes, *sir*," she agreed happily and went away to the kitchen.

"Dammit, you can't just *move in*," I said crossly.

"Why not?" he asked in surprise, demolishing hot cakes swiftly. "I happen to be very fond of hot cakes, next to light rolls."

"You're fond of anything edible," I retorted, "and at the rate you're cleaning my larder, I can't afford you."

He grinned at me disarmingly, and reluctantly I grinned back. "How quickly could you pack, Bi?" he asked, suddenly serious. "I think you'd be safer at the ranch. Could you make a five o'clock plane?"

"Safer—from *what?*"

"Whatever's going on."

"And what will you be doing?"

"Why don't I stay here a few days," he reflected. "I'll keep an eye on the place, see what turns up with the man next door, while I'm running down leads for Ludo."

Well, what a delightful idea, to be sure! Get rid of

me entirely and search the place at leisure? I thought
drily. All my uncertainties returned. I'd only Perryn's
word that what he wanted were the notebooks; he
wouldn't have told me that, if I hadn't caught him in
the cellar—but on top of George turning up next door,
perhaps it was a prearranged meeting?

"Oh, no, thanks. I have to water the roses at five."

He looked at my ingenuous face and snorted. "All
right, there's a plane tomorrow. I'll put you on that;
the estate agent will meet you in Albuquerque."

"Really, thanks but no thanks."

He looked at me sharply and evidently thought he'd
got it. "All right, if you don't fancy the idea of your ex-
brother-in-law's ranch, why not visit your brother in
. . . wherever he is?"

"Maracaibo," I murmured, "and I fancy the idea of
that even less."

"Of all the stubborn little donkeys," he began
violently, but Peace Beloved banged open the service
door to set a fresh plate of hot cakes on the table, and
perforce Perryn shut up.

She shook the coffee pot vigorously, sending a large
splash on the fresh tablecloth. "Ooops," she remarked
lightheartedly, "there *was* enough coffee after all," up-
ending the pot over his cup until it was swimming in
the saucer. "Think I should make some more?"

"No, thanks, this is plenty."

She studied him carefully as he began on the pancakes, and I noted a faint languor in the wielding of
knife and fork. "You *sure* you is right full up to the
top, Mr. Perryn?" Peace Beloved demanded in a no-
nonsense voice. "Those litty-bitty pieces of hot cake
is bouncin' around, hittin' the bottom of your elimin-
ary canal?"

Perryn choked slightly and took a quick sip of coffee, while I met his eye with gentle interest. "Peace
Beloved, your price is far above rubies," he said fi-

nally, "and if you feed me to the point I can't get into my existing wardrobe, rubies is what it will take to buy a new one."

"Aw, I ain't all *that* virtuous, Mr. Perryn," she chuckled blithely, swishing back to the kitchen, where she hurled everything full force into the sink (judging by the sounds) and crooned "Yeah-yeah-*yeah!*" while running water like the cataract of Lodore.

I broke apart at the blank expression on his face, and eyeing my shaking shoulders, he broke up, too. We sat there like a couple of idiots, gasping with laughter, until finally he said, "My God, Binks, no one but you would ever wind up with such an insane maid! Where in hell did you get her?"

"She goes with the house," I said, controlling myself, "she bird-dogs the tenants on Polly's behalf, but she don't has to watch me because I is family."

He looked at me, the bright blue eyes suddenly still and intent as he fumbled for a cigarette. "*This* is why I don't believe it," he muttered half to himself, shaking his head absently. "It's—the same as always, only more so."

"I don't fit the concept of Mata Hari, do I?"

He shook his head violently, squinting through the smoke. "I never knew you very well, that's what threw me off," he said reflectively. "You were beautiful, brilliant with the brains; you directed things far better than Helen ever did; you made yourself liked by society in general and the staff in particular.

"And Ludo adored you," he mused. "That was good enough for me . . . so when this exploded, I didn't stop to reason, when the FBI was so positive." He flicked ash into a tray and eyed me impassively. "But it now occurs to me, Binks sweetie," he remarked with a faint twitch of the lips, "that my initial estimate of you was: 'For a bright girl, she's terribly stupid!' "

"Julian says I need a keeper," I admitted in a small

voice. "He says I'd mislay my head if it weren't tied on, and he thinks the string is too loose."

Perryn smiled *en passant,* and pursued his analysis. "That first Christmas," he narrowed his eyes, "so help me, I sat there literally flabbergasted at the calm way you were prying Rafe and Helen from their cozy little nest . . . and making it smooth as cream, totally uncombatable. At the time, I admired your naïve sweetness; as of now, I realize it was the McCoy, and Ludo knew it, even if I didn't."

There was a final grand slam of cabinet doors in the kitchen, and Peace Beloved burst into the dining room. "Closets?"

Perryn pushed back his chair and stood up. "Do them alone?" he said charmingly. "I need to talk over family business with my—cousin. Come on, Binks. Peace Beloved doesn't need you breathing down her neck."

"No, *sir,*" she agreed heartily, eyeing me sidewise. I got the message.

"Yes, you may take the radio with you, but if I hear even half a Beatle, off it goes, understood?"

"Yas'm, Miss Robinson," she said happily and crashed away to the cellar, while Perryn winced involuntarily.

"How's the ankle?"

"Tender but bearable," he said, walking toward the living room with only a faint favoring of the left leg.

It was one of the rare days. "Let's sit on the porch." I dragged the heavy chairs away from the doors and squeakily turned the keys, while Perryn watched silently.

"Do you always barricade at night?" he limped forward to sink into one of Polly's luau chairs.

"No, of course not," I said surprised. "but last night was when I first saw George—and now I think of it, who knew his name?"

"There was a slip: Ask your wife about George."

"But who *is* he?" I asked desperately. "I'm positive I never met anyone named George Crosson in my life, Perryn."

"Is that his name?"

"If he's 'Uncle George'," I shrugged. "Didn't the FBI find out *anything?*"

"They weren't looking into George," he said, "and I told you, they wouldn't tell me anything. I suppose I can't blame them, but actually they only egged me into spilling the beans. If they'd told me *anything*, I'd never have come here, I'd never have heard your side."

"You think I *have* a side?"

He nodded soberly. "You haven't the wits for this sort of double play—sorry, Binks. I'm told you're suspected of treason; *I* find you within two days, living with no attempt at concealment, exactly where you'd be expected to be—with a cat, a maid, and a rose garden. You'd have to be Sarah Bernhardt if you meant to lie low this way—and Divine you may be," he grinned at me fleetingly, "but Sarah you are *not*.

"I know this the instant I really think about it. Ludo would have known it, too, except for his emotional involvement. The FBI won't know it without proof, so that is what we will arrange to give them. Get me a pad and pencil?"

I got the telephone table jotting pad, hearing Peace Beloved thrashing about overhead, solaced by muted Beatles. "Why were you so sure I had Ludo's books? If he thought I'd abused the information, wouldn't he instantly have taken them back? Why aren't they on the boat with him this minute?" I asked.

"A good point," he said, "and I'm *not* sure, Bi, but Esther says they were still in the study the day you packed your papers."

"That was a full week before the case was heard."

"Ludo *never* came back to the house . . ."

"He'd have sent Victor, then."

Perryn shook his head. "He was with Ludo on the boat. Esther went over each night and came back in the morning. No," he said, "I think the FBI persuaded Ludo to leave the books—*so they could watch what you did with them.* They wouldn't admit anything, but I got a distinct impression of satisfaction when I inquired—sort of 'everything's going according to plan.'

"So I came down on the off chance the place names might *not* be in code—and you produce this *wild* story, accusing Ludo, plus all sorts of innocent explanations for everything else." He shrugged. "Let us now have facts. What can you prove and how?"

"Helen will back me on the furnishings," I said slowly. "If they won't take her word, some shops would be sure to remember us. We got her silver at Nils: four dozen of everything, and she wanted it marked a special way. It isn't a big shop; don't you suppose they'd recall it?

"There was a set of Havilland china from a Parke-Bernet auction . . . and the kitchen equipment came from Le Cuisinier," I said hopefully. "It was the biggest single order they ever had, the manager waited on us himself, and we took most of it with us in a taxi, direct to the apartment." I chuckled at the memory of the doorman's face when we drove up and had practically to be dug out from the middle of the packages!

"Did *you* pay, or give Helen cash and *she* paid—or did she deposit your checks and draw her own?"

"I cashed the checks before we started out," I told him vaguely, "but I usually gave her the money so she could *seem* to be paying. Once or twice, I think I went alone to pay for something we'd already ordered."

"My God," he said in a startled undertone, "were you running around town with twenty thousand bucks in your wallet? Why didn't you simply draw checks as you went along?"

"Miss English," I said in a very small voice. How

explain that combination of avidity, prying, unspoken censure? Miss English was an office version of Miss King. "She *pounced*," I looked at Perryn pleadingly, "and she *questioned*. She always wanted to know what every check was *for*. If I'd written checks to Helen— or to shops for china and silver—she'd have asked *why*, or where the stuff was."

"Why not say 'None of your damn business'?"

I hung my head. "That's one of the things I'm not very good at."

"And you never told Ludo you were scared to death of the old harpy, because you knew she'd been with him for years?" he nodded his head. "All right, *I* understand—but *now* do you see how it's not wise to be considerate of unpleasant characters? *You* protected her—but the instant the FBI talked to her, do you think she protected *you*? Not on your life! She had a ball, telling them about those unexplained checks for cash!"

"Why didn't Helen tell them?"

"I don't suppose she was ever asked, Bi. They only talked to her once, and she said flatly she didn't believe a word of it," he said absently, scribbling notes on the pad. "I think it's a tragedy of shut-mouths, Binks . . . because if the FBI were right, it'd be serious as hell.

"Look: Rafe knew about the information leak; he never saw the pictures. David saw the pictures, but didn't know about the information leak. The telephone operator tipped me the FBI talked to Miss English; neither Rafe nor David knew *that* . . . and she only admitted what she'd said because I gave her the idea I was merely verifying what the FBI had told *me*.

"So now we come to your book . . ."

"That's easiest of all," I stood up and simultaneously Peace Beloved (and Beatles) crashed into the study overhead. "Everything's in one of the cartons downstairs."

"I think I shall come with you," Perryn grinned. "She has a light hand with hot cakes—and the heaviest feet I ever heard!"

I went swiftly to the cellar, with Perryn behind me. "Sit on the stairs," I suggested, tugging at the cartons. "There isn't any chair down here, and I don't know which box it is. They certainly *sealed* these things. I'll have to get a knife."

Perryn fumbled in his pocket and tossed a silver-mounted jack-knife toward me. "Decide which carton you were going to open last, and do it *first*," he advised.

"Bet a dime I get it first crack!"

"Not unless I choose which one you open," he objected.

"All right. Which d'you pick?"

He poked his head under the railing and considered. "*That* one," and I slit it open obediently, pulled back the flaps and right on top was the publisher's contract.

"Dime, please!"

"I picked it, too," he said indignantly. "Bet's off."

I was too triumphant to quibble. "See," I tossed the contract up to him, "it says the advance they're to pay, and it's exactly the same amount. We could certainly get a photostat of the cancelled check to prove it was the deposit to my account on that date." While he scanned the paper rapidly, I rooted out the carbon copy. "Here's the book itself," I began, as Perryn glanced down to the open carton.

Clutching the manuscript to my chest, I could feel the blood draining from my face while Perryn muttered, "Well, that's par for the course!"

Neatly arranged beneath the book carbon were Ludo's diaries . . .

"But I *didn't!*" I cried frantically, bursting into tears.

"Hush, of course you didn't," he said, letting himself down the remainder of the cellar steps and limping

over to pick up one of the notebooks. "Stop crying,
Binks! If I'd ever needed a clincher, this is it. Would
you happily open a tightly sealed carton before my
very eyes, if *you* had packed those things, sweetie?"
He tossed the book back into the carton and squatted
beside me, patting my shoulder soothingly, while I
gradually calmed down from boo-hoo to sniffles. "Who
packed these boxes?"

"I did. There were professionals for clothes, but I
sorted personal papers and left the books on the
study table." I gulped forlornly remembering those
unhappy days.

"Who sealed?"

"The packers. They brought special cartons for
books," I nodded at the larger-sized boxes, "and
sealed and labeled—but I'd already gone to the St.
Regis with Julian."

"It could be just a mistake," he murmured. "The
packers thought you'd overlooked something and
Esther didn't know the diaries weren't yours." He
stood up and turned to the steps. "Bring the notebooks."

I collected the things and followed him to the
living room. "Please, let's call the FBI!"

"Not yet," he said, absently.

"Why not?" Unwillingly, I felt a faint return of suspicion. He'd wanted the diaries; I'd led him to them.
Was Perryn now trying to figure some way to complete his mission—hampered by a sore ankle? Did he
really not know where Ludo was—or perhaps knew
perfectly well, and it was part of Ludo's plan to retrieve the books, leaving me still under a cloud?

"You have the most speaking face, Bi," Perryn
chuckled. "You're wondering if I mean to scoop 'em
up and dash for it, aren't you?" He threw back his
head with a shout of laughter. "Quit it, sweetie!"

"Then why *not* call the FBI?"

He stopped laughing and sat up. "Because," he

said soberly, "there have to be other phone calls, and I still need a clue to Ludo's whereabouts. Once they get their hands on those diaries, only Ludo can get them back. So we will *first* extract everything useful. Are all the books there?"

I stood them on end, using my hands for bookends. How dumb can you be? I'd thumbed through them off and on for nearly three years—and I had no idea how many there were!" "He'd have the current one on board, but I can't remember if there were ten, or eleven, or only nine old ones," I confessed miserably. "I'm sorry, Perryn."

"Can't you tell by the dates?"

I shook my head. "The entries only say August—or Monday—and where he was. Ludo didn't need exact dates."

Perryn snorted with exasperation. "It's going to be a hell of a job," he muttered.

"What?"

He ignored me, thinking hard. "Would I get Esther if I call New York now?"

"Yes." I glanced at the clock: nearly four. "If you're planning to stay, I have to market."

The blue flash of Trael eyes flicked over me blandly, as Perryn stood up. "Yes, *cousin*," he said gently, "I shall be here—*until Ludo gets back to look after you.*" He plucked a fifty-dollar bill from his wallet, folded it and stuck it neatly into the top of my blouse. "Buy roasts and lobsters and steaks and things," he suggested.

"What will you be doing?"

"It occurs to me I have a car on the next block, containing luggage. I shall hobble over, bring it back, have a decent shave and a clean shirt. Peace Beloved can count the silver before and after . . ."

"Oh, she don't has to watch you," I returned absently. "You forget: you is family. I'll drive you around," as he snorted irrepressibly, "and she'll let you in when you get back. What do you want for dinner?"

"Chateaubriand?" he said instantly.

I shook my head. "They don't understand beef," I said apologetically. "I patronize a supermarket with Green Stamps, and it's more slanted for the family trade than gourmet. Is there anything you *won't* eat?"

"Fried oysters, baked beans and parsnips," he said in a peculiar tone of voice. "If you had the right steak for Chateaubriand, could you cook it, Binks?"

"Of course, if I knew the stove," I said, surprised, "but this one seems to have a mind of its own." I went upstairs, found my handbag and told Peace Beloved I was going to market. "Listen for Mr. Perryn, he'll be back in a few minutes—and if you're ready to leave before I get back, I'll pay you tomorrow, or ask him—I only have large bills."

"Yes, ma'am, Miss Robinson," she said cheerfully. "My, this was a *nice* day, wasn't it?"

Well, for some women (of whom I make one) any day is a good day if it has a man in it. "Yes, it *was* a nice day, Peace Beloved . . ."

I found Perryn in the kitchen, bent over the shopping pad with a faint frown. "What'n hell are we having, Binks?" I peered at the list and translated.

"'Tower pepper' is paper towelling, Ajack is cleanser, and Tinkle is a copper cleaner for the saucepans," I said impatiently. "Come on, or they'll be shut before I get there." He was still holding the list when I ran the Volkswagen out of the garage, and as he jack-knifed into the front seat, he thrust the paper at me.

"Here—and if 'cancon' turns out to be a nautch girl, I won't be at all surprised."

"I will," I remarked austerely, "because it ought to be a steamed corn pudding. Which way to your car?"

It was nearly six before I got back. Peace Beloved was still there, getting ready to leave by very gradual stages, which apparently consisted in lingering in the living room archway and unburdening her heart to Perryn. He was comfortably ensconced in the biggest wing chair, his feet on the ottoman and supplied with a bar tray plus a substantial snack. At a glance I realized he had Ludo's light touch with servants and Peace Beloved asked nothing more than to wait on him hand and foot. Unquestionably, he'd elicited every blessed thing she knew about me and my life in Chevy Chase—which would only confirm my blameless existence, and bully for my side!

"You is *back*, Miss Robinson?" Peace Beloved inquired.

"Yes, this is me," I said, "and if you don't get a wiggle on, you'll miss the six-thirty bus."

"It don't matter; they's another at seven," she shrugged. "I'll help you unload and put away. I hopes you got more tacos and pattyfoy; I used all you had for Mr. Perryn." She looked at him fondly.

"And very good it was, thank you, Peace Beloved," he said blandly, as she trotted away toward the back driveway. "I hopes you got more tacos, too; extremely good!" He munched appreciatively. I laughed at him, helplessly.

"As a matter of fact, I did—but that's all the pattyfoy there is, which rules out Tornedoes Rossini, if you were wanting any."

He shook his head. "I'm happy with anything at all, provided there's enough of it," he said indistinctly. "Go deal with the food, and for heaven's sake get rid of her."

That was easier said than done. Peace Beloved was deeply interested in each item. By the time I'd explained what I meant to do with the tripe—*and* the sweetbreads—*and* the veal kidneys—and received expert advice concerning chitlings (which I had somehow failed to purchase), it was well after six-thirty. "Thank you very much, and *now* you must leave," I said firmly, "but you can come back and see him again tomorrow morning."

"Yes, ma'am, Miss Robinson," she said amenably, and crashed away to the front door. "Well, good night, Mr. Perryn. See you-all tomorrow. I is good for breakfasts, but Miss Robinson is better for dinners. Whoo-*ooo*, you sure is going to like your vittles tonight!"

"Good night, Peace Beloved," we chorused politely, and while the front door was still shuddering from impact, the transistor radio wafted a full volume of Beatles to our ears . . . gradually diminishing up the street toward the bus stop.

We looked at each other silently for a moment, and broke apart simultaneously. Perryn laughed until he was holding his sides and writhing in the wing chair. Finally, he sat up and wiped his eyes. "There was never a girl more inaptly named: *Peace* Beloved," he observed feebly. "She makes more noise than a launching pad. Sit down and have a drink, Bi, and let's relax."

It was an attractive suggestion. I spread a few crackers with "pattyfoy" while Perryn fixed highballs, and we sat, chatting idly, as though the FBI didn't exist. The wind was rising, the sun had nearly set; I got up absently to shut the porch doors—and noted a spot of color. "Oh, heavens, the roses! I promised Suzanne to water them. Have another drink and play cat's cradle or something for half an hour?"

"Take your time," he said, polishing off his drink and setting the glass on the tray. "I still want to make some phone calls, Bi; you don't mind?"

"Of course not."

I went hastily out to the garden tap and turned it on, ducking away from the water spray and tracing the thing to the nozzle; it was the sort of hose you have to regulate by hand. When I suggested a sprinkler, Suzanne's expression stated clearly that I had sunk in her estimation. "Roses need *different* kinds of watering," she told me, firmly, and as she was in charge of this chore, I felt if she wanted to cope with a spray nozzle, let her.

Tonight I stood patiently, directing the water to each separate bush, and automatically counting buds as I moved along the bed. There was three half-opened red and white buds, and two fabulous pale pink roses, fully spread and scenting the air for yards around. While I bathed the roots neatly, not letting any water touch the leaves for fear of spots (as ordained by Suzanne), I debated: to cut, or not to cut? Reason said she would instantly miss those roses upon her return; on the other hand, by Monday they'd be passé. I felt slightly furious with Providence for permitting those roses to bloom at the exact moment when Suzanne, who'd brought them into being, should be away.

She'd worked so hard, loved them so passionately, and the first reward arrived when her back was turned. In the gathering dusk as I shifted to the other side of the bed, I tried to put myself in her mind: would she rather I left them to be overblown, but at least for her to *see*—or would she understand if I cut and enjoyed them in the house? There were obviously going to be quantities of roses; the red and white ones would be lusciously open by Monday—but *these* were the *first*.

By the time I'd completed the circuit of the bed, I'd decided: cut, enjoy—and with any luck, plus a bit of sugar and Clorox, they'd still be fresh enough for her to examine on Monday. I turned off the tap and made for the toolshed and secateurs. It was full *crepuscule* by now, and something was banging gently in the evening breeze.

Instinctively, I peered around. Julian's house was warm with lights, but there were no shutters and as all the doors were warped, requiring main force to

open or shut, this pleasant zephyr was certainly not
banging anything at my place. Nor was it on the other
side, toward Miss King . . .

*It was the cellar door at the bottom of the cement
back steps of the house next door . . .*

Inevitably, I found a way through the privet hedge,
at a thin spot behind the garage. I acquired a number
of nasty scratches, and my heart was pumping furiously. What did I mean to do, what would I say if I
were seen? That I had merely come to shut the door,
knowing the family was away—and had stepped inside to check the possibility of a burglar?

A likely tale, my mind jeered. What unaccompanied
young woman would be so brave? And suppose there
really *was* a burglar? Looking at the door, I knew it
wasn't forced; it had been hastily closed and the lock
had not quite caught. I went quickly down the steps,
pulled the door open and stepped into the house.

It was pitch-black and completely silent. I stood
for a moment, determinedly recalling Peace Beloved's
description of the basement: a bedroom and half-
bath, a recreation room, big storage closets, a section
for the oil heater that also held the laundry. My eyes
were dark-adapted now, and I could dimly see that I
was standing in the rec room. Feeling my way across
to the stairs leading to the kitchen, I boldly flipped
the switch. I still didn't know what I hoped to find—
some clue to George, perhaps.

The big room was evidently Suzanne's play area,
with books and games, tidily stacked on shelves.
There was a shabby old couch, with a tasteful arrangement of photographs on the wall above. Unconsciously I studied them: quite beautiful work,
landscape shots printed on rice paper. I felt a thrill
of pleasure to recognize a superb view of Gemlik
looking toward Istanbul, and another of the harbor at
Manila. The others were not readily identifiable—a

flotilla of sampans that might be anywhere in the Orient, an oddly stunted tree that was Japanese in feeling, a country waterfall . . .

All the pictures were signed "Lavretta." I made a mental note to inquire about him at the art shops. I rather yearned for a print of the Gemlik picture to give Julian and Polly, as a reminder of the summer they came up from Kuwait and met me in Athens. We'd taken an Aegean cruise, stopping here and there, and going overland from Bursa to Beirut.

I suddenly realized I was lingering far too long and hastily continued the inspection tour. I found the utility room, two store closets filled with bags and trunks, and finally the bedroom, which was in the corner and apparently didn't have a ceiling light. I could just make out two doors for bath and closet, and a pin-up lamp above the single bed. Absently I turned it on, and found the bath was the first door.

I've no idea what made me open the closet. Expecting nothing but empty hangers on a pole, I'd nearly closed the door before I realized there was something else in that closet.

I flung open the door again—and a dull red glow bathed the interior automatically.

It was a complete and very professional photographic darkroom.

I stood in the doorway, feeling my blood congealing, and simply *knowing* Ludo's pictures had been rigged in that very spot. I backed away, as from a king cobra, and shut the door carefully. In my search, everything had been so normal as to lull fear; now it was all back and I was wild to be away from the place. I was nearly out the door when I realized I must turn off lights. Racing back, I had my hand on the switch of the pin-up lamp, glancing back automatically to estimate unfamiliar distance to be covered in the dark. I was also facing the painted wooden chest, and upon its top was a silver-framed portrait.

Helen?

Impossible!

But it was unmistakably Mrs. Ralph Trael, wearing a cocktail suit from Dior. The photograph might be black and white—but the suit was a heavenly shade of raspberry red, in a soft nubby wool with a seductive neckline that was not-quite-off the shoulders and banded with sable. It had cost $850, and I had been with her when she bought it last September . . . shuddering dramatically at the price and saying humorously, "Thank heavens, it's *red*. Rafe will pay for *anything* so long as it's red!"

If I'd needed any further information, there was the Maria-Theresa necklace of intricate gold chains strung with dewdrop diamonds, peridots and rubies. It was an expensive bauble, but authenticated. It had cost a thousand dollars, and I'd found it in Paris as Helen's birthday gift from Ludo and myself, last summer. She'd been enraptured with it, and Ludo said privately I was a clever puss to get it for so little, as the diamonds were rose-cut instead of eight-points, as I'd thought. The deciding factor on ordering the cocktail suit had been, "It will be *perfect* for the necklace, Binks."

The photograph was superb: Helen at her best and most beguiling, a hint of smile at the lips, a warmth in the expression of the eyes. I held the photograph in my hands, smiling in sad reminiscence . . . such a lovely woman, such a good companion . . .

And what was her photograph doing here, framed in silver, printed on rice paper and signed Lavretta?

I replaced the thing and fled, turning off the lights and slamming shut the cellar door in my haste.

Julian's house was ablaze with lights, and I could hear Perryn calling urgently, "Bi? Binks, where are you? *Bianca!*" I thrust my way through the hedge, to stand shivering beside the wood pile. Insensibly, I had been relaxing; unconsciously, I had been thinking everything was in a way to be straightened out, that it was only a matter of time, with Perryn to help . . .

And now—how could I trust anyone, anything?

Behind me the garage light went on, the the kitchen door crashed open, and Perryn was making his way painfully down the path—swearing violently as he stumbled on the garden hose, and bellowing importunately, *Bianca!*

I took a deep breath and emerged into the glare of the bulb. "Yes?"

"Where have you been?" he demanded, limping forward to grasp my shoulders and half-shake me angrily. "Dammit, one minute I can see you watering the roses—and the next it's full dark and you've vanished." Even while he was speaking, I'd made a plan. I would tell him *everything*, apparently accept whatever glib explanations he offered—I was sure he'd have an answer for everything—and I would then telephone the FBI and *tell them everything* . . . and demand they either permit me to go to Julian and Polly, or find me a secure hiding place under their protection. I should have known I couldn't avoid the searching intuitive Trael gaze.

"What is it?" he said. "What's happened? Are you hurt? Where'd you get those scratches? Did someone attack you? For heaven's sake, Bi—*where have you been?*"

I shook myself free of his arms and stepped around him. "I've been in the house next door," I said calmly, "and I have to start dinner now."

Chapter
7

I was browning floured meat by the time Perryn had hauled himself up and into the kitchen. He sat on the stool and opened his mouth with a fulminating glance, but I beat him to it. "*Not* while I am cooking," I stated, dragging scissors and flashlight from the gurry-drawer and thrusting them at him. "Go out and cut the two *pink* roses," I ordered, casting brandy into the pot and setting a match to it—whereat the kitchen apparently went up in flames. Perryn shouted, "Stand back, Bi. I'll have it out in a minute. Dammit, I thought you could cook . . ."

"I can—and *I* will have it out in a minute alone and unaided," I said crossly, fending him away from the stove. "*Go* and *get* the roses before I lose track of where I am." He turned away distrustfully and I could hear him swearing when he stepped on the hose *again*. Arthur had emerged from his afternoon siesta and from prior experience was sitting wisely in the dining room, peering around the door jamb.

"Hell. You'll get your dinner as soon as this is started."

"Mmmwow," he said in his 'take your time' voice.

It was only when dinner was under control, table set, Arthur coping with cat chow and ice bucket re-filled that I realized Perryn was taking an unconscionably long time to cut a measly two roses. Peering from the dining room window—sure enough, I could see flashlighted movement circling the basement next door.

Silly ape, I thought irritably. *If he doesn't rook the other ankle in the dark, one of the neighbors will be bound to report a prowler to the police.* I nearly went out to drag him home, when he vanished around the back corner looking into the bedroom. I knew Helen's picture faced the window; would the flashlight be strong enough to identify it? I wondered, sickly, what Perryn would dream up to cover it. I knew now he was a clever devil, a good match for Ludo, well able to lull stupid Bi! Returning to the kitchen and stirring the meat, I wondered *why* I had to be lulled.

It was more than mere divorce; Ludo *did* know he had only to ask . . . because he knew I was too dull-witted to refuse. Had he thought a shrewd lawyer might ask more on my behalf than I'd ask for myself? He could still have got me to sign a waiver before-hand . . . or persuaded me to be represented by a man of his choice. After four years of living with me, Ludo *must* have known exactly how dumb I was, how easily I could be played upon, to agree to anything.

He might have had the photographs and evidence ready—in case there were a slip-up in court—but there hadn't been one, and he'd used it anyway. *Why?*

Because I was a most useful scapegoat for some-thing much more serious? I smiled to myself grimly. I was finding out altogether too much for comfort, due to Perryn's being caught in the cellar. All the sweet talk, about Ludo's deep love for me . . . all the busi-ness of Perryn staying to protect me until Ludo came home . . . I'd believed it because I *wanted* to believe it.

Still—he hadn't *had* to tell me about the FBI, un-less he was afraid *they* were going to tell me? He'd said, "Divine you may be, but Sarah you're not," and by the same token, I couldn't visualize Perryn as a Laurence Olivier, to play this part so convincingly. The one possible explanation to fit all circumstances was that *Ludo* himself had leaked that important information. I rejected that without a second thought; *perhaps* Ludo could really think *I* was a traitor. I simply knew *he* wasn't; not even necessary to think about it. For one thing, he'd have had so many opportunities long before he married me . . .

I couldn't think about it any more, because Perryn was coming in with the roses. "Here," he dropped scissors and light into the gurry-drawer while I found a vase in the corner cabinet. "Did you say you were *in* that house next door? How'd you get in?" he asked abruptly.

"The back door was banging in the wind."

"So now you have neatly locked it. Dammit, Bi," he said exasperated, "why didn't you call me?"

"You were phoning," I faltered, unconsciously apologizing.

"All right," he sighed, turning to the living room. "Let's have it: what did you find?" He replenished drinks as I sat silent, but there was no avoiding it. The mere delay in reply told him there was something to tell.

"There's a complete photographic darkroom in the bedroom closet," I said starkly, "and—a picture of Helen on the bureau."

Perryn's face was stunned. I could swear his bewilderment was genuine. "*Helen?* Are you *sure?*"

"She's wearing the Dior suit and Maria-Theresa necklace."

He took a long swallow of his drink. "It was a photograph, not clipped from a magazine?" he asked, presently.

"It was a photograph, printed on rice paper, framed in silver, and signed Lavretta like the others."

"Others?" He pounced at once, and made me explain the landscapes on the rec room wall. "Well, it could make sense; she's forever being photographed for the papers," he said. "Either George is a friend of

Lavretta's, who got a print of a picture of a beautiful woman he may or may not ever have met . . . Was it autographed?" I shook my head. "Or George is Lavretta himself, which is much less good, because then Helen knows him."

I opened my mouth, but he held up a hand, "But, if Rafe never saw the pictures, Helen certainly didn't," he mused. He looked at me squarely. "Binks, would you—could you—bear to look at them carefully? I pried a set out of Anscot, and it took some doing, I can tell you! But you keep saying they were rigged. Could you prove it, in some way?"

"It *was* my dress and negligee . . ."

"Those could have been borrowed." He drew a folder from his breast pocket, tossed it into my lap and limped away, murmuring something about "Need a handkerchief, upstairs . . ." On the bottom step, he turned and said strongly, "Don't *think* about them, Bi! *Analyze* them—understand?"

I nodded, but it wasn't easy to be so impersonal. There were twelve shots. Two seemed in a nightclub where—apparently—I was cuddled and smiling against George's shoulder, and in one of them I was obviously drunk, judging by the squinty vague eyes.

There were three showing me in a diaphanous peignoir that was definitely all that separated me from the breezes. Again, George and "I" were smiling blearily at the camera, and in one, his hand was apparently laid on my breast, disarranging the robe to reveal a long seductive expanse of bare leg, while "I" clung to him with a drunken leer.

The rest were simply filthy: seven pictures, with a bed and George in underpants, while "I" was stripped. The poses were nauseatingly suggestive. In every picture my face was clear, although George was half-turned and not entirely identifiable—unless you'd seen the whole package—from which anyone would deduce it was he.

I let the things fall into my lap, tears blurring my eyes, hearing Perryn moving overhead—giving me time to prove or disprove. I blotted my eyes with the cocktail napkin and deliberately picked up the first pictures again—and something *did* strike me.

I completely forgot positions and clothes, and compared the drunken nightclub shot with the drunken peignoir picture—and unless I was insane, *my face* was exactly the same in both! Furthermore, I had a vague recognition of that picture, and Ludo roaring with laughter . . .

"Hey!" I shouted to Perryn. "Bring the magnifying glass from the desk, I think I've got something." He came crashing down the stairs, two at a time on the good ankle, and thrust the glass at me.

"What?"

There was no doubt: the two faces *were* the same. "If only I could remember," I said, as Perryn bent to compare, agreeing, "You're *right*, Binks, there's no question! They took your face from some old pictures and transplanted with a model!"

And then I remembered.

The publisher of *First Clues* wanted "informals"— and Ludo undertook candid camera of me at work in the study. Heavens, we'd had *fun* that afternoon! He did a full roll of black and white, as well as color, very seriously and carefully, producing a dozen excellent shots, to the publisher's astonished glee. Then it was drink time; Victor brought up a tray, and was impressed into service to hold the flash. Esther innocently came looking for Madame to be dressed for dinner and the opera—and wound up perched on my desk, directing a floodlight downward. We'd grown sillier by the minute, with Ludo pretending to be a Hollywood director, and me, writing a script as we went along, until Victor and Esther were giggling too, with consequent wobbling of lights.

When the film was developed, there were the good

shots, and a second string of "not bad"; the rest were ridiculous, mad, absurd. We put them in my "press book" with captions by Ludo . . . *and the face in these pictures was the one of me, sitting at the typewriter, holding high my drink, and somehow Ludo'd pressed the button exactly as my eyes were half closed* . . .

I sat silent, feeling sick to my stomach, while Perryn was still bent over the magnifying glass. I'd been right all along. It was Ludo himself who'd hired George Lavretta to fake those pictures. It was suddenly clear to me: wanting out, he'd met Lavretta through Helen—bribed the man to create the evidence, given him the old negatives from which to use my face. No wonder I wasn't let to examine closely! I thought cynically. Ludo would *die* when he learned how the pre-honeymoon silence had led his brothers into tipping the wink to me!

Steadily now, I picked up the nude photographs. These were the ones the Court had agreed only Ludo could verify—and he had done so, which only went to prove how anxious he must have been to get rid of me *to have overlooked a small but very present appendectomy scar!*

I had one.

The body in the photograph was unblemished, but for a vaccination mark on the arm.

My vaccination was on the right thigh . . .

So now I *knew*, and I must be *very* careful, because if Perryn realized what I'd learned, he'd destroy the pictures to protect Ludo. The similarity of heads didn't matter; what mattered vitally was the nudes. They mustn't be endangered. I had to have them—so I could go to any doctor, even a policewoman, and prove that no matter what the face looked like, *that body wasn't mine!* Swiftly, I slipped the two pictures to prove my point beneath the seat cushion, returned the rest to Perryn. "Here. I'd better check on dinner."

Starting water for rice and vegetables, my mind

squirrelled wildly. Did I still have the press book? It would be in one of the other cartons. I got a sharp knife and whizzed down, to slash open the other cartons—and in the bottom of one, I found the green leather binder.

"What more?" Perryn asked quietly from behind my shoulder. I should have remembered he had Ludo's panther-walk. "Something that involves Ludo, of course," he murmured, squatting beside me. "It's revived all your original suspicion, to the point you've hidden two of the pictures." He took the folder from his pocket and extended it. "Don't you know these are only copies, that Anscot would never give anyone the originals? I could burn 'em all, and your lawyer could get another set from AVT tomorrow.

"Anscot's *very* twitchy," he remarked, "and you are going to tell me *why*. Yes, you *are*, sweetie," he stood up and extended a hand to pull me up beside him, "but first we will dine—and we will chat of cabbages and kings, until digestion is complete . . ."

Arthur joined us at table, sitting sociably on a side chair and resting his nose on the cloth, occasionally turning to blink affectionately at Perryn, who rapidly went through two plates of *osso buco*, accompanied by rice and three helps of salad, before the sigh of repletion. "Coffee in the living room?" I suggested, scraping veal bones into Arthur's dish. They'd be dragged anywhere, including the front entry, but Arthur adored *bones,* particularly if he could chew on them when I was nearby.

On impulse I went down and dug out the press book. I was going to put the whole thing in the lap of the FBI, after all. Perryn might as well know what I was going to say, to prove.

He eyed the book thoughtfully when I tossed it next to the pile of Ludo's diaries. We drank coffee with Benedictine, and listened to the usual uninspired

Boston Symphony TV menu for the hinterlands, which proved to be a mishmash of Mozart's Hafner teamed with Til Eulenspiegel, of all things.

"Esther says the diaries were there *after* you left," Perryn observed quietly. "She's certain, because the study phone rang as she came back from seeing you into a cab. It was Helen, and when Esther said how nearly she'd missed you, Helen cried . . . but Esther remembers the row of black facing her as she talked.

"Then she dismissed the packers for lunch, went down for her own. When the men returned, she led them to the study—but she had to supervise the men finishing your dressing room. *Now* she recalls the diaries were gone; she noticed the gap between the bookends, and remembering how you loved the cat figurines, she stuffed them into one of the valises . . . but with so much to do, so much emotion, she didn't question . . ."

He smiled faintly. "She was immensely relieved to know *you're* all right. She hasn't heard from her husband, either . . ."

"*I* don't have a husband," I told him evenly. "Poor Esther, she must be frantic!"

"David's still trying round the clock," Perryn ignored my comment. "There's a crumb: Egyptian archaeologist named Falmy, here for a scientific congress, dropped in at the office. When David said Ludo was out of the country, Falmy said he hadn't really expected to see him—*because he'd seen the Ariel going through Suez about a month ago.*"

"But if *he* saw the Ariel, why didn't Interpol find it?"

"Exactly. I begin to think the FBI knows where Ludo is, but if so, they're idiots not to say," Perryn remarked grimly.

"They *don't* know where he is," I said flatly. "They may be clams but they are not idiots, and when you're obviously going to stir the pot, they'd give enough to shut you up—if they had it."

"I suppose so. I missed Helen and Rafe; they'd already left for the evening. Now," he said, "what is that book?"

Silently I found the squinty picture and handed the press book to Perryn. He got it at once. "Ludo took this?"

"Yes."

"Mmhm. Are there any other faces you recognize?"

"I don't know; this was the only bad shot we kept."

"Where were the negatives?"

"How should I know?" I asked helplessly. "Ludo had them. He gave the good ones to the publisher. I don't know about the others. I'd have thought he would throw them away."

Perryn sat back, silently leafing through the press book and returning to the picture under which Ludo's neat engineering script had lettered, "It'll get you every time." He smiled absently, and closed the book. "Why did you keep the two pictures?" he asked softly.

"Because I could go to any doctor and prove that body isn't mine," I said after a moment, not looking at him, "and after four years . . ." I couldn't go on.

"You think Ludo perjured himself?" Perryn finished. "He should have known it wasn't you, but he testified under oath that it was?"

"Yes," I whispered.

Surprisingly, Perryn laughed. "Binks, use your head!" he said. "That's another clincher! You know Ludo. He's a very brilliant, very careful, engineering brain—who would *never* have made such a boo-boo if he'd been in charge! What was missed?"

"I have an appendectomy scar, and a vaccination on the leg, not the arm."

"I don't suppose he ever really *looked*," Perryn said thoughtfully. "He saw the face and the nudity—and if it hadn't been combined with the information leak, he wouldn't have been fooled." He sat frowning. "Binks —don't be insulted—but did you ever have a fleeting impression that something was *peculiar?* A sense of— oh, being pressured, not for money, but an implication that you *ought* to do something for favors received?"

"You mean, I'm so dimwitted I might never have realized someone was trying to blackmail me?" I translated.

He grinned ruefully. "More or less. You're obviously mentally left at the post when it comes to the wickednesses of the world." He leaned forward to stare at me compellingly. "Think! Was there ever anyone who was disproportionately huffy when you refused to help, someone who made snide remarks along the lines of 'you'll be sorry'?"

I thought for the space of a cigarette. "That's the worst of being stupid," I said finally. "You don't get it at the time, so how can you remember it later?"

"All right," he said with a smile. "Forget it for now. The important thing is a transcript of the diaries."

I was totally rocked by his matter-of-fact tone. "*Why?*"

"I want to know where Ludo is likely to have gone," he said as if explaining to an idiot child. "Dammit, he's my *brother*—and Africa's a powder keg today. *I* can't read the things; will you, for heaven's sake, leaf through and give me the names of all the African places he's been—so I'll know where to look for him?"

It sounded logical. I would still call the FBI, but I could see no harm in giving Perryn place names. If he had an ulterior motive the FBI and Interpol would be onto him before he could do any damage.

I picked up the first volume to hand, and quickly realized they did fall into a sort of order. The first time Ludo went any place, he described it fully; succeeding visits only amplified existing knowledge, em-

phasized technical data, mentioned people re-en-
countered, and were filled out with legends and folklore. "You only want Africa?"

"Yes. That much the FBI admitted, and Falmy
confirms, if the Ariel went through Suez."

Ludo hadn't gone to Africa every year, which
meant tedious leafing through several of the notebooks
only to find he'd been in Scandinavia or Colorado. I
could feel my eyelids drooping with weariness, while
Perryn sat alertly over the yellow pad, making notes.
"Take a break and get some coffee," he suggested.
"I'm sorry to put you through this, Bi, but you do see
how we're getting something?"

What we got was three full pages of names, and
Perryn wasn't through. "Where are these places? Is
there an atlas?" I found it and we bent over the page
for Africa. "I can't see Zimbabwe?" he complained,
fretfully.

"Southeast of Victoria in the Upper Mtetkwe," I
said absently, positioning the magnifying glass and
pointing. "About—there. It won't be on the map."

"Why not?"

"It's a prehistoric Phoenician fort," I explained
kindly. "What's called Ophir in the Bible, but the
Egyptians got there first and called it Punt. That's
where they got their gold."

"I see." He tossed the pad to me. "Where's Ludo
gone, Binks?" Perryn asked in a peculiar tone, and
when I stared at him, startled, he smiled at me. "You
know more than you think you do," he said. "What's
there, that could be vital, that Ludo's gone to find?"

"Not Madagascar," I said slowly. "He was there
only a few months back . . . mostly quartz and tourma-
line, good for A-bomb test gauges, but not enough for
an 'incident'."

"Gold—oil—diamonds—?"

"He wouldn't know about oil; he's a mining engineer," I reminded Perryn. "Anyway, Julian says there

isn't any to speak of. He and Polly were in Inhambane before Barsa, and if *Julian* says it isn't there, it isn't there."

"No, we're not thinking clearly," I said suddenly, holding up my fingers and absently ticking off points. "It has to be something valuable that nobody knows is there—*not even really Ludo.* There has to be enough to be worth extracting for market. It has to be something he only noted in passing—and the international incident is that whoever deciphered the entry has now sneaked in with an exploration contract, or bought the land at a worthless-value price." I looked at Perryn, who was gazing at me in fascinated silence.

"What and where is it?" he asked in a strangled voice.

"Not gold in Rhodesia," I reflected. "Everyone's known about Gwelo and Selukwe since the Bible. Not Tanganyika; Williamson found the diamond pipe." I studied the list of place names again, and debated aloud. "Was it something he ran across at a fueling stop, or something he noted on a real trip?"

I sighed with the frustrated realization that even if I made a verbatim transcript of every word Ludo had written about East Africa, I hadn't the knowledge to pick out a particular item to cause an international incident. Was there any other way?

"It *isn't* any of the British Colonies," I said, with relief, "because there might be a miff but there wouldn't be an *incident.*" I studied the map again. "For choice, it's Mozambique," I decided. "Either the Limpopo or the border of Lake Nyassa."

"In heaven's name, why?"

"We said it's something valuable nobody knows about. Suppose there's workable gold to the south— or diamonds to the north? The Portuguese Government's had enough trouble with Angola to be pretty fond of Mozambique, no?" I shrugged and sat back to light a cigarette, while Perryn studied the atlas.

"You've got it, of course," he said presently. "I expect Lisbon would take a very dim view of anyone turning up in control of potential riches." He snorted sardonically, and threw his arm about me in a convulsive hug. "Binks, you've a *frightening* intelligence for some things!"

Not the right things, I thought sadly. I was a woozy-headed little lamb being led to the slaughter. I'd been so catched by research and deduction, I'd been *lured* again . . . into telling Perryn exactly what he wanted to know.

Arthur was peacefully snoozing, draped over my ankles and evidently adjusted to the concept that we were sleeping down here tonight. As Danny had said, he was a very *good* cat. I scrambled awkwardly to my feet, picking him up into my arms. "Hadn't you better go to bed? You remember Peace Beloved is serving breakfast at eleven?" And long before then I would have called the FBI . . .

"Yes," he sighed, pushing the atlas aside, "and I wonder why I ever hired her."

"Because she is making light rolls for your dinner," I told him austerely, and went up to bed.

Chapter
8

Sunday was a *most* unusual day, to quote Mr. Rod-gers.

Peace Beloved arrived, *sans* Beatles. They were not, it seemed, suitable for the Lord's Day. When I suggested that *all* days were the property of the Lord, the concept was beyond her.

She'd unearthed Polly's waffle iron and set the light rolls to rise by the time I tottered downstairs at noon. "Figure brunch for one; Mr. Perryn and I were up late."

"Family business," she nodded placidly, producing two cups of strong black coffee, one after the other, while I sat over the Sunday *Times*. I'd finished the Double Crostic and was coping with the crossword before Perryn joined us. He was resplendent in an Austrian shooting jacket of the largest, loudest checks ever seen. Arthur and I shied involuntarily, but Peace Beloved could hardly take her eyes off him for admiration. "Whoo-*ooo*, mmmh-*mmm*, you is mighty sharp today, Mr. Perryn," she breathed respectfully.

"Thank you, Peace Beloved. I rather fancy it my-self."

"Aren't you afraid you'll frighten the game?" I asked, but he only grinned and applied himself to waffles, while she trotted back and forth, happily supplying fresh waffles, melted butter, hot coffee, crisp bacon and syrup.

I looked at my ex-brother-in-law, tucking into a

superb Sunday breakfast, with a perfectly clear face,
a happy eye, and plenty of gusto—and I *knew* it was
no act. Whatever Ludo might have done . . . and I
remembered Perryn saying, "I'm bound to admit he's
too close-mouthed"—Perryn was unaware of it.
Whether or not Ludo would thank him for taking
care of me, I suddenly absolved Perryn of any hidden
motives.

"I've been thinking," he said presently, "and I'd
better go myself, Bi. The FBI and Interpol are no use;
they're so sure it's you, and we haven't enough yet to
sway them. But I want you out of here! It's just luck
you haven't been recognized," he rode over me when
I started to protest. "Don't you see, at the moment
we've got the drop on George. I want to keep it that
way. If only you hadn't locked the door!"

"That's me," I said fatalistically. "I never think *first*
about anything. That's why," my lips trembled, "I
wasn't surprised Ludo got bored with me . . . but I
didn't think he had to do it this way."

"And now—don't you realize *he* didn't do it at all?"
Perryn countered softly, "and I don't believe he was
ever bored with *you* for a single second," he added
with a hearty laugh, pushing away from the table and
going to the kitchen, where I could hear his bare-
faced flattery producing rich giggles.

Arthur and I transferred ourselves to the side porch.
Perryn called, "I'm going to phone David," and went
up to the study. It was still a most *unusual* day. I
polished off the crossword, with long intervals of
thought between clues . . . and I could *not* make myself believe Perryn was playing a concave suit. I
couldn't make myself believe Ludo was a traitor,
either. Possible that he might somehow have been
lured into the rigged pictures in order to get his freedom; I was well aware Ludo was capable of ruthlessness . . . but I'd never (I suddenly remembered) seen

any sign of ruthlessness except in the sense of righteous retribution.

He was capable of blacklisting a native who maltreated animals, or failed on the job. He didn't stand for petty thievery of supplies, nor inefficiency that might endanger a safari three days' march in the bush . . . but similarly, for the honest native, Ludo had understanding, sincere praise, the sort of *camaraderie* that produced near-worship for Bwana Trael . . . Sahib Trael . . . El Senor. I'd seen it time and time again when I was with him.

So if he'd demolished me in court, Ludo had thought it, quite literally, his *duty*. More and more I thought perhaps Perryn's story *was* credible . . . and that he would straighten it out, as soon as he found Ludo.

I lay on the porch lounge, contemplating roses in Sunday stillness, Arthur snoozing in my lap, and Peace Beloved softly singing "Deep River" over the breakfast dishes . . . and drowsily I joined my cat in the arms of Morpheus . . .

I woke to find Perryn quietly turning pages of the paper, the sun slanting low, and Peace Beloved tiptoeing out with the bar tray, well stocked with crisp hot tacos and a plate of bubbling cheese dreams.

"You is *awake*, Miss Robinson?" she inquired earnestly.

"No," I said straight-faced, pulling myself to my feet. "I am somnambulistic."

"Nicely timed," Perryn remarked judicially, fixing my highball while Peace Beloved stared at me uncertainly.

"You *is* awake, Miss Robinson," she assured me.

"Miss Robinson is awake, but not very," Perryn soothed. "That will be all, thank you, Peace Beloved."

She backed away, eyeing me dubiously, and I felt slightly ashamed of so confusing her, but Perryn was extending my glass, and it was slooping dangerously as his shoulders shook with suppressed laughter. "I know," he murmured, "sometimes you can't resist! If you haven't a sister, how about a cousin, Bi?"

"I haven't one of those either," I suddenly realized the time. "I have to water the roses."

"That's where you vanished yesterday!" He set down his glass and accompanied me firmly, rambling about idly while I adjusted the spray. "I missed Rafe and Helen; they'd gone to the boat races," he said abruptly. "David thinks you might be right, he's alerting someone in Lourenço Marques. If we've heard nothing before, I'll get the noon plane to Lisbon tomorrow—put down in Cairo and Nairobi, and if there's still no word, go on to Lourenço Marques—*if that's where I should go.*"

He looked at me expressionlessly. "But is it, Bi? There's a thousand miles of bush, if I pick the wrong end. I could waste two or three weeks, checking dead ends and getting to the other spot." His blue eyes held me mesmerically. "You want him back," he said softly. "Work it out for me, Binks? Where do I start?"

You want him back? Of course I did! "I'll get him for you," Perryn said softly. "Tell me where he is Binks . . ."

I moved to the end of the rose bed, considering. "He was never on the boat, of course; he put in at the nearest port in Europe and took a plane," I said suddenly, "leaving the boat to follow because it wouldn't be fast enough. If Falmy saw the Ariel at Suez a month ago, she'd reach Mozambique a week to ten days later—and she needs a deep harbor. You can't hide her in an estuary. So if she isn't openly berthed somewhere—which could be *anywhere,* simply as a red herring," I inserted despairingly, "she fueled and stocked at the last possible moment—but *not* where Ludo was really going, of course.

"Mombasa, perhaps—or Zanzibar, Dar es Salaam . . . Then she could cruise for a month to six weeks—

by anchoring off shore every night to save fuel." So I
was ruining Ludo's careful scheme by perception? But
suppose it *wasn't* a scheme? Suppose it was legitimate,
and there'd been an accident . . . and Ludo was ill,
somewhere in the bush? I caught my breath. I
couldn't take any chance of that, and the possibility
that I might save him by playing my end straight.

"He'd have to show a passport to any airline,"
Perryn said presently. "Why didn't Interpol turn it up
by now?"

"Because they're looking for the Ariel," I shrugged,
"and they probably *do* know where she fueled, but
then they'd lose her again, if she's simply hanging
around off shore, waiting to meet Ludo at an agreed
rendezvous. Holt knows every drop of water on *Earth*
like the back of his hand; he could keep out of any
ship lane for as long as his fuel lasts, Perryn."

"Yes," he agreed. "All right. Where is Ludo, Binks?"

"He went to Salisbury by plane," I said slowly,
working it out in my mind, "and from there to the
Sabi by bush plane. I think he has to be heading for
Sul do Save, because he's spent more time in that
area," I looked at Perryn apologetically, "because
Zimbabwe was important to me. Ludo went every
time he was nearby, to make scale drawings and take
photographs. Isn't it logical to suppose he spotted
something in passing?"

"It *isn't* gold," I realized with a frown, "because
anyone would sort of expect to find that, and it would
long since have been worked over. No, it's some other
ore, valuable because there isn't too much of it, which
would make it worth plenty in terms of foreign ex-
change for a government." I dropped the hose at the
end of the bed.

"Why should Ludo *vanish* because of it?"

"He went to see if it's really there," I said in surprise. "He felt responsible, of course, so he's told whatever government it is that he'll make a private sur-

vey—and that's why he hasn't even told David . . . to prevent any possibility of a leak. Don't you see? He's *protecting* everyone by lying doggo. If he doesn't talk to *anyone*, there *can't* be any accusations." I went to turn off the tap, and came back, ruminating. "Of course, Ludo *knows* what it is. Tin, I shouldn't wonder; there isn't much, and I think the Patinos have most of it."

"I thought you knew nothing about mining?" Perryn observed, while I wiped my damp fingers on the hem of my slip.

"I don't—but *anyone* can go from A to B," I said, blankly.

"Shall we try for C—and perhaps Z?" he suggested. "Ludo went to Salisbury, wherever that is, nearly two months ago . . ."

"Capital of Rhodesia," I said absently, "and of course he never thought it would take so long." We went back to the house, where the kitchen was fragrant with baking "light" rolls. "I should do something about dinner," I remembered, but Perryn pushed me firmly to the living room.

"Later. First we finish Sherlocking." He thrust me into a chair and retrieved the drink tray from the porch. "Why wouldn't Ludo know exactly how long it would take?"

"Because he wasn't a free agent. First he had to confer with people in the other government, and probably it all had to be approved in Washington."

"The Bureau of Red Tape and Sealing Wax," Perryn muttered. "Yes, that figures. He'd expect to walk in, say where he was going, and walk out—and instead there was a week of argle-bargle. It still leaves six weeks, Binks."

"He had to waste a little time in Salisbury, doing the pretty while he arranged on the side," I said, pulling the atlas open once more. "Then he took a bush plane to Victoria, and put together porters and supplies—but he was always fussy, Perryn, and he'd be twice as fussy now, to get men he knew he could trust implicitly.

"And some were in the bush on safari, so he waited till they came back," I said thoughtfully, "but it has to be some place he *thought* he could make and return in a month . . . so it's about ten days from Victoria."

"It couldn't be so far," Perryn objected, looking over my shoulder intently at the map. "Even if everything went on greased wheels, that'd be three weeks for the round trip, Binks, and he had to allow time to get there in the first place."

"Oh, *he* wouldn't go back," I said kindly. "Ludo went on to the nearest place—it could even not be a settlement, there's plenty of veldt in Mozambique— where a bush plane was waiting to take him to the coast. He could make it in two days, and if you want the Ariel—" I looked at the map again, "she's hanging around between Beira and Inhambane, hitting Mambone every night after dark—waiting for Ludo's signal."

"Good God," Perryn muttered, studying the map. "If you're right, he could be nearly finished and back to home plate," he said. "Once on the Ariel, he'll contact David."

I shook my head. "Not until he's delivered his official report—and suppose," I shivered involuntarily, "he isn't let to reach the Ariel? If it's important enough to create an international incident, it's worth a knife in the back."

"You've been seeing too many Late Late shows," Perryn scoffed. "If Ludo found villains, he'd only have a bigger ball for himself, crawling through underbush on his belly and outwitting them." He leaned over and hugged my shoulders, just as Peace Beloved emerged into the hall and surveyed us fondly.

"I is going home now," she announced. "You leave

the dishes, Miss Robinson; I do 'em tomorrow, but if I waits now, I lose the last bus. The Sunday schedule is different."

Perryn got up lazily and abstracted ten bucks from his wallet. "Treat yourself to a cab," he suggested, "and put the rest in your piggy bank as a thank-you for giving up your Sunday. And get here as early as you can tomorrow, because I have to go to New York and I'm sending Miss Robinson to New Mexico until I come back."

Both Peace Beloved and I were inclined to argue the point, but Perryn merely stood erect and said, "Now *hear* this . . ." so we heard. Peace Beloved was to come every day to take care of the house and play with Arthur, so he wouldn't feel nobody loved him—and I was to sunbathe on the patio and tell Minnie to teach me how to make a tamale pie.

Peace Beloved agreed instantly, of course, although obviously slightly surprised. "You don't like her here alone, Mr. Perryn, but she *been* alone for two months and ain't nothin' happen to her," she stated for the record.

Perryn tapped the spigot marked "charm" and sprayed her with a smiling blue flash. "But I didn't know she was here alone, Peace Beloved, and now that I do—I won't be easy in my mind unless I know someone's with her," he said, rumpling his hair in boyish distraction. Peace Beloved capitulated like a sitting duck.

"Yes, *sir*, Mr. Perryn," she agreed wholeheartedly. "Miss Robinson, she much too pretty to be alone—and you don't worry, I'll take care of Arthur. I wonder," she mused, "would he like some beef heart? I could pick it up easy, on my way to the bus."

"I'm sure he'd relish it, but please don't spoil him!"

"He's going to need plenty sweetening, if you go away," she stated flatly. "When you comes back, he be so glad to see you, he don't ask for nothing else!"

When finally she'd gone, I turned on Perryn, but he only raised his eyebrows. "There's a plane at 2:30; you're on it," he said quietly. "No nonsense, Bi! We still don't know about this Lavretta. I want you out of sight and reach." He put his hands on my shoulders and held me facing him. "No use for me to find Ludo—and lose you." He smiled, but his face was sober. "I'll be off first thing in the morning, turn in the car at the airport. I've wired Drummond to meet you."

"What about the FBI?"

He squinted into space, reflectively. "I'll phone them in New York," he announced, "to say *I* have sent you to the ranch . . ." He smiled faintly. "They didn't help me; I don't think I shall help them—beyond letting them know *I* know where you are." He looked down at me reassuringly. "It won't be long, Binks," he said softly. "Let me look for Ludo with an easy mind about you, please?"

I could only nod and unconsciously bend forward to rest my forehead against Perryn's chest. "Haven't you got a stepsister or a third cousin?" he complained, lightly.

"No, but—" I had a sudden flash, "I have a niece . . ."

"Good Lord, I'll be doddering on a cane by the time she reaches the age of consent," he guffawed, slapping my shoulders and releasing me. I had my mouth open to tell him Phebe was twenty-four years old, a Smith graduate *cum laude*, currently a small but important wheel in a computer planning study group—and always causing grave concern to Julian and Polly because she was as vague as I. I never had a chance. "What's for dinner?" asked Perryn. "And if you think that's a broad hint—it is."

Rustling about the kitchen, I was suddenly aware of lights next door. "They came back about half an hour ago," Perryn said calmly. "Did you think I wouldn't be watching? George simply let them off at the curb and drove away."

Peace Beloved's light rolls were feathery; Perryn ate seven—plus three chicken quarters Dijon, most of the salad bowl and still found room for strawberries in wine. He was a very big man. I only hoped Polly had taught her daughter to cook . . .

He'd gone by the time I got downstairs next morning, and Peace Beloved was back to Beatles and *"Yeah-yeah-yeah!"* "Good morning Miss Robinson, it is a nice day for flying," she said cheerily. "You want me to help you pack?"

"I can manage, thanks." I realized there were things to think about. "Use up the food in the fridge, Peace Beloved . . ."

"Ain't much left. Mr. Perryn ate the rest of the rolls, and all the eggs and bacon . . ."

"Then you'll have to get whatever you need for yourself. I'll leave money—and if I give you a check for salary, could you get it cashed?"

"Mr. Perryn, he paid me," she shook her head. "He say you don't think about *anything* but pack and get the plane. He left a letter for you, on the table."

It was terse. "Binks—*get out of town!* I'll pay your ticket on my way through the airport. *A bientot!*" There was a hundred bucks in assorted bills; Perryn had apparently thought of everything, and insensibly I relaxed. He was right, of course; I mustn't run any risk of complications now. The instant he found Ludo, Perryn could either make him *listen* to my story . . . or Ludo would be forced to admit *his* chicanery . . .

I looked up absently and met my own eyes in the hall mirror. *Do you really think you married a stinker? Do you really believe Perryn is playing a deep game?*

Well, I might be stupidly naïve, but the instant answer was *no*. Furthermore, looking at myself, I knew quite certainly that if I were wrong, I wouldn't care whether I lived or died. If I could be *so* fooled, after four years of marriage, I didn't deserve a future . . .

Believe, and play it straight. Vaguely, as I folded clothes suitable for the ranch, I thought I would retrieve my rings en route to the airport. Vaguely, I wondered what Ludo was looking for . . . which instantly brought the notebooks to mind. *I* ran downstairs. Sure enough: *there they were!*

What would be safest, I debated. Leave them here or take them with me? They wouldn't fit the deposit box; would the bank have a larger size? That meant time: to phone Lennart, before I took them with me —more time to sign for another box, deposit the books. It was already noon, and I had still to dress and finish packing. No, it was take them to the ranch, or leave them here . . . and suppose my luggage were searched on the plane? Perryn had said he'd tell the FBI where I would be, but would he have told them we'd found the diaries? I thought not; I thought it was the one time he'd forgotten—to agree what we should do with them.

On the other hand, only Perryn knew for sure the books were here. Even if the FBI could search while Peace Beloved was away, it should be unsettling to discover the diaries *here*, when *I* was two thousand miles away! On the theory of the Purloined Letter, I made a space on the lowest darkest shelf and neatly aligned the notebooks next to a stack of National Geographics.

I'd wasted fifteen minutes on this; if I meant to stop at the bank for my rings and make Dulles Airport in time to pick up my ticket, I'd have to hustle. I hustled. I was just locking my suitcase when I heard the unmistakable sound of a taxi. Bethesda taxis have a damnable intercom system to alert drivers for calls —and make any trip miserable for the occupant. *Impossible* to believe Peace Beloved's Beatle-brain could

cope with a telephone, let alone order a taxi at the
correct moment on her own responsibility? Could
Perryn have planned so well for my comfort as to be-
speak a cab for one o'clock?

Incredulously, I stared from my bedroom window.
It was an airport taxi, and it was not picking me up,
but decanting a feminine figure.

Helen . . .

She was wearing an apple green linen redingote
lined with an enchanting violet printed silk matching
the sheath dress beneath. As she followed the driver
toting a suitcase, her eyes flicked up and over the
house with an expression of happy anticipation.

She's going to the ranch with me, I thought joy-
fully. Oh, *bless* Perryn to have thought of it. I was
running down stairs as the bell rang. "I'll get it, Peace
Beloved," I called, flinging wide the door. "Oh, *Nell*
—this makes everything complete!"

"Binks!" she said, half-crying. "I couldn't wait! I
just *threw* things into a case and came the *instant*
Perryn said you were here all alone." She hugged me
softly. "Oh, I've been absolutely *wild,* not knowing
where you were, but Perryn was so *relieved* when I
said I'd stay—and Rafe sends his love, and you're not
to worry about a thing. Heavens, isn't it going to be
fun?" She drew back with a long breath of satisfaction, stripping off her gloves and smiling at me mist-
ily, then looking about her. "Are you *really* living all
alone in this funny little house, sweetie?"

"It belongs to my brother," I said automatically,
while Helen walked into the living room, abandoning
gloves and purse on a chair, as though there were all
the time in the world—which there definitely wasn't
if we were to make the plane to Albuquerque—but
apparently that wasn't on her agenda. I suppressed a
rueful smile. Obviously Perryn had thought I'd dis-
obey, so he'd prepared a second line of defense! Rather

a joke on him that I'd been docile—but actually even nicer to have Helen with me again.

Swiftly I rearranged my plans. I never had wanted to go to the ranch; with Helen here, I could stay out of sight fairly easily. There remained Peace Beloved. "Let me tell the maid—and we'll have to market," I said eagerly. "Perryn ate me out of house and home."

I went rapidly down to the cellar where Peace Beloved was coping with the washing machine, and said, "I'm not going after all; Mr. Perryn's sister-in-law has come to stay with me, instead, but will you still come every day, please, and make up his bed with fresh linen and towels in the bathroom?"

"Yes, ma'am, Miss Robinson," Peace Beloved said placidly. "That's nice, you don't have to go away. I be up in a minute to fix her room."

"Where *are* you, Bi?" Helen complained gaily. "I want to see everything. Where do I sleep?"

Oh, it was nice to have Helen to talk to—although there was a tiny shadow of constraint. That is, we gabbled like mad, but we both skirted the divorce and everything pertaining thereto. There was no mention of Ludo, or pictures or information leaks, and only the most glancing reference to Perryn's having found me.

Just as well, I thought while I found extra dress hangers and told Helen lightly, "This is do-it-yourself! I have a maid for the rough work—that's all."

"Heavens, I *trust* I'm capable of hanging up a dress." Setting the contents of her dressing case on the bureau top, she regaled me with an account of a disastrous dinner party at the Abercrombies that had me laughing until I cried—but in the back of my mind I already knew I wouldn't say a word of what Perryn and I had figured out. He'd said this was a complication of everybody knowing something and nobody knowing everything. I couldn't be sure how much Helen knew. She seemed not to know Perryn had actually stayed here for several *days,* for instance, or was on his way to Lisbon right this moment—but perhaps they wouldn't tell her that because it would lead to mentioning the diaries. It was even possible Helen didn't know Ludo was missing, rather than simply away. Best to say nothing about anything . . .

We went to market, and it was more fun than ever before, with Helen discovering unfamiliar items and commenting wickedly on things and people. She was enchanted by the Green Stamps. "I'd heard of them, of course, but I never knew anyone who collected them."

"You should speak to your staff once in a while," I returned calmly. "*Esther* was saving for a mink stole, I believe."

"You mean, my servants patronize *supermarkets?*"

"Of course," I nodded, "and privately I prefer trading stamps to kickbacks, wouldn't you?"

"Heavens, yes! The bills are high enough as it is," she shuddered, and eyed me admiringly. "However did you dig this out?"

"By accident," I giggled at the memory. "I saw some luscious apricots; I bought some; I got some Green Stamps—and when I got home, Esther took them away from me."

Helen burst out laughing. "Oh, *Binks!* How long before she gets the stole?"

"Not too long, I fancy. She had Victor trained to fuel the car at a station giving stamps, and I *think* she'd found a dry cleaner and shoe repair in the racket, too."

"What d'you mean to do with yours?"

"I shall get a wall can opener that *works,* as a house present for my sister-in-law," I said instantly, eyeing the baskets marked "extra coupons" and realizing we could *always* use floor wax, even if already well supplied. I got two cans, and a hundred extra stamps—

and looking at the things sitting smugly in my basket, I accepted the fact that I must have a middle-class mind, after all. As always, Helen entered wholeheartedly into my spirit.

"There's a special on stuffed shrimps," she announced, coming back from one of the aisles while I was scanning the meat display, "and *immense* bags of potato chips, but I rather like them with drinks, don't you?"

"The shrimps are no good," I said absently, "I fell for them once before. I think the only way they can get rid of them is with bonus stamps—but get two packs of chips; Peace Beloved likes them, too. Shall I get chicken breasts or thighs—and what about a slice of ham to bake?"

"White meat for me," Helen hung over the counter beside me. "Pork tenderloin! How about Chinese sweet-and-sour, if I can only remember Hsu Chang's directions—the most *divine* little Chinaman, Bi! Hissing kin . . ." she said straight-faced, and left me snickering over the meats.

The red and white rosebuds had spread themselves to the afternoon sun. "Why don't you take them?" I suggested to Suzanne. "The pink ones opened while you were away, so I cut them. I hope you don't mind, but I had company."

To my great relief, Suzanne didn't mind. She looked with critical approval at the pink roses, absorbed my instructions on bleach *cum* sugar for keeping petals fresh, and happily agreed to take full charge of the bed while my "cousin" was staying with me. "That is," I said artfully, "unless you'll be going places with your uncle?"

She shook her head. "He's gone back to New York," she observed disdainfully. "I wish he'd stay there. He only comes here to take pictures."

"He's a photographer?" I asked, *very* casually.

"Yes. All he did all weekend was take *pictures*," she muttered, kicking her shoe against the lowest back step, and looking at me with sudden defenselessness. "I had to put on a zillion different bathing suits and run in and out of the waves," she said, unhappily. "It's going to be a TV commercial or something—but the money is to send me to college, so I guess it's all right."

"Of course," I agreed. "How nice to have a famous uncle to photograph you, Suzanne!"

"He isn't famous," she said contemptuously, hopping away on her private game along the back path. "Mama says he's a bum, even if he is her own brother, and she doesn't like him to use me for a model. Well, so long, Miss Robinson."

"So long," I said, retreating into the kitchen and closing the back door thoughtfully.

"Who was that?" Helen asked. "What about a drink? Can I help with dinner?"

"That was my rose gardener, aged eight and happy to learn she's in full charge so long as I have company," I said. "Drinks coming up—and what in hell do you know about dinner?"

"Nothing," said Helen. "I decided at the age of fourteen, when I was embroiled with the domestic science course at Miss Madeira's—that the simplest way to a happy marriage was *not* to be able to cook. Then any man who married *me* was going to have to buy me a cook, or starve to death—and if he could afford a cook, he could probably afford other things as well."

"Diamonds, Dior and *de luxe*," I giggled, "but you *do* know how to set a table; silver in the side chest . . ."

Helen was even better than Perryn; she had a critical palate, and her wide-eyed praise was heartwarming. "I ought to hate you, Bi," she said soberly. "You're a complete woman and I'm—nothing. You can

SEASON OF EVIL 151

write a book, or sew a button on your husband's shirt, or cook," her voice sank, "or have a baby, even if it's fussy—but I can't even do that."

"So what? You have other qualities, sweetie," I said, keeping it light. "Coffee *and*, in the living room? Benedictine, chartreuse, what you will?"

"Benedictine," she decided, and smiled at me brilliantly. "I *can* carry cups," she stated, and picked them from my hands.

I set coffee and liqueur on a tray, turned for glasses and realized there were lights in the kitchen next door. "Who's George Lavretta?" I asked in a by-the-by tone, as I set the tray beside Helen.

"Lavretta?" she repeated blankly. "He's a photographer, Binks—if it's the same man. I used him for portraits a few years ago—competent, but not exceptional," she frowned in memory. "Why? If you want pictures, I have a fantabulous woman on East 62nd.

I looked at her graceful wrist, delicate pink-tipped fingers, pouring liqueur into our glasses without a tremor, and nearly said, *How come there's a silver-framed portrait of you on his bureau if you don't know his first name?* But as Perryn had pointed out, it wasn't signed—not the first time a man framed his secret love in silver, unbeknownst to her—and Helen was a beautiful woman.

"I saw a photograph at an exhibition, I'd rather like a copy," I said glibly, "and you're the expert on photographers. I thought perhaps he was a Big Name."

She shook her head, kicking off her pumps and propping her crossed ankles elegantly on the ottoman. "Ask the gallery," she suggested indolently, and launched into an account of the opening night at Easthampton.

Slowly, the conversational circles narrowed until finally Helen looked at me squarely. "What really happened, Bi?"

"I don't exactly know, even yet," I said slowly, "and

I don't want to hash it over . . . except Perryn believes me, too."

"Too?"

"Well, *you* believed me; I mean, you didn't even know what happened, but you flatly *didn't* believe I was a bitch," I said, warmly, leaning over to crush out my cigarette. "There's one thing you can do to help, when the times comes: verify that I paid for the furnishings of the apartment. Apparently, there's a moot point about what I did with all that money. Of course, we can get some of the tradesmen to remember, if necessary, but . . ." My eyes swept up across Helen's face. "What's the matter?" I asked, startled. She was lying, half-collapsed against the couch, her face so ghastly pale that every touch of make-up stood out like a clown's mask.

"No!" she said harshly. "I—Binks, there has to be some other way!"

I stared at her, astounded. "There isn't any other way. It isn't a Federal case, sweetie." (Although of course that was just what it was, come to think of it.) "Not testifying in court; just confirming I bought the stuff for you." She was still tremulous and I thought of Perryn's comments. "Rafe?"

Her eyes darted over me and studied the floor, as she nodded, silently.

"He gave you money to furnish, and you lost it—so he never knew I paid for everything?"

After a moment she nodded again. "Well, it's a case of does Macy's tell Gimbels," I remarked, "because *you* thought Rafe bought the place."

"He *did*," she said startled.

"Oh, no, he didn't. Ludo had to buy it for him," I chuckled. "Rafe was 'temporarily embarrassed', too."

Helen stared at me and when I nodded mirthfully, her face suddenly broke apart, and we both laughed fit to kill ourselves. "But why is it so important, Binks?" she asked. "I mean, it was a hell of a bind at that point, but I could give it all back to you in a couple of mouths, if you need it."

"No, it isn't that. I don't want the money; I only need you to say that was how I spent it—and don't worry, I'm positive Rafe needn't ever know." Her color returned slowly, but I still felt *odd,* even while I was chatting about odious Miss King. I'd never been afraid of Ludo; I couldn't imagine a woman ever being afraid of Perryn—but perhaps Rafe was different.

Later, as we went sleepily up to bed, I thought—if Helen could lose fifty or a hundred thousand dollars of her husband's money, Rafe might be justifiably angry. Still, it should be possible, since the FBI had been stupid clams this far, to clobber them into being intelligent clams, once Helen had privately confirmed my story. Ludo would have to know, but it was not necessary to tell Rafe—and it was all in the family, after all.

I could hear the snick of Helen's light switch, the faint motions of settling, and finally the gentle breathing of sleep. I curled on my side and stared into darkness, feeling a tremulous happiness. I had Helen to keep me company, while I waited for Perryn to find Ludo; I had Peace Beloved to wash dishes, and (with a *plop*) I had Arthur to warm my toes. I yawned comfortably, and contemplated my niece as a sister-in-law. On the whole, I thought Phebe would do nicely for Perryn, although it was going to louse up the Trael genealogy if I wound up being aunt to my first cousins once removed . . .

Chapter
9

If Helen only knew Lavretta "several years ago," how come his portrait of her is wearing a dress she only bought last fall? said my mind as I woke next morning. I lay thinking for a moment, ending in my usual frustration: I couldn't recall exactly what Helen had said. Was it "a few years ago" or "for a few years?" And now she'd found a fantabulous woman on 62nd Street, which was Helen to a T. Every news agency had stock shots of Society names, some so outdated as to be ludicrous—but there were up-to-the-minute glossies of Helen four to six times a year, whereby the "beauteous Mrs. Rafe Trael" got three or four times as much coverage as any other Society girl . . .

I stretched lazily and abandoned the subject. I rolled out of bed and peeked at Helen, who was still dead to the world, as I tiptoed in, adjusted blinds and softly shut the door. Throwing on some clothes, I trotted downstairs just as the telephone rang.

"Long distance calling Mrs. Trael."

"I'm sorry, she's still asleep; who is calling, operator?"

A harassed male voice interrupted, "Mrs. *Bianca* Trael? This is David Corey— it's all *right*, operator, put the call through at once, please . . . Mrs. Trael, are you there?"

"Yes."

For the first time in all our acquaintance, David was irascible. "*Why* are you there, Mrs. Trael? Why are you not at Casa de Burlas? Mr. Drummond has met every plane, he is worried to death!"

"Oh, heavens!" I'd completely forgotten Perryn's estate agent.

"Will you *please* take this afternoon's plane, Mrs. Trael? I've made the reservation—2:30 from Dulles Airport."

"I'm so sorry, but I forgot all about it . . ."

"You *forgot* about . . ." David's voice was strangled. I knew at once he would never get over the shock that his boss's wife could *forget* a jet plane—and candor compels the admission that jet planes are not easy to overlook, but I am the sort of dilly who can do it.

I pulled myself together and made an effort, for Ludo's sake. "Well, I was just about to leave when Mrs. Trael arrived," I apologized, "and I thought perhaps Mr. Perryn had sent her to go with me, but she didn't seem to expect it—and then we got to talking and somehow neither of us went. I'm so *terribly* sorry, should I call Mr. Drummond and tell him the plans are changed?"

"Mrs. Trael?" he said in a stunned voice. "You mean —Mrs. *Ralph* Trael is with you?"

"Yes—so I don't think I'll go to New Mexico after all. You may as well cancel the seat," I said, grasping the phone tightly. "Oh, David—*is* there any news yet?"

"There's nothing I can tell you, Mrs. Trael," he said in his "official" voice. "Oh dear, I don't like that *at* all," he fussed. "Mr. Perryn said *definitely* you were to go to the ranch. He said *nothing* about Mrs. Rafe; in fact, I understood they were in Southampton, but if you say she's with you . . ."

"She is," I assured him.

"Perhaps you should *both* go to Casa de Burlas," he said hopefully. "Oh no, that won't do; I got the last seat on the 2:30 plane for you—but there's another at . . . let me see . . ." I could hear scrabbling papers.

"No please. I'm sure she wouldn't like it, and I

wouldn't like it either," I said soothingly. "Leave it as
it is, David. I'm perfectly safe, and if you're in touch
with Mr. Perryn, tell him Mrs. Rafe is with me and I'm
being careful. He'll understand what I mean—and
David, you *will* let me know?"

He was silent for a long moment. "The instant there's
anything to tell, you'll know, Mrs. Trael," he said,
warmly "unofficial." "I promise!"

How had I spent time before Helen came? It hadn't
dragged, between polishing Polly's pots and silver to a
sparkle, supervising roses, rehemming the living room
draperies that some cleaner had returned in a boggle.
Occasionally I found a late movie dating from the days
when Hollywood still produced entertainment. The
ceiling-to-floor bookshelves were crammed with everything from paperbacks to poetry, and I had the germ of
an idea for a historical novel. I'd been leisurely-busy
enough to avoid thinking, until I achieved the compo-
sure of a vegetable, but it was a bucolic existence un-
known to Helen.

It was all too true: she didn't cook, or knit or em-
broider, or play solitaire, and even with Peace Beloved
every day, there were chores. I wracked my brains for
possible amusement. When Helen finally came downstairs for coffee, she protested, "Heavens, I didn't expect social life, Binks! I only came to keep you company, because Rafe said Perryn was so worried. Now,
don't feel I'm a *guest.*"

But in such a small house, I couldn't help but feel
awkward to abandon Helen to a book while I was pre-
paring things in the kitchen, or typing a sudden idea for
the novel, particularly as Peace Beloved was so over-
awed by Helen's elegance that she was making every
effort to rise to the occasion. Gone were Beatles,
"Yeah-yeah-yeah" and all her joyous friendliness to
Perryn; she was efficient as always, but silent, nor
could she bring herself to say "Miss Helen." If Helen

spoke to her, she said "Yes, Mrs. Trael," or "No, Mrs.
Trael," as required, but she kept glancing at me, as if for
approval.

It was enormously touching, but also a terrible
strain, and after a couple of hours I was amazed to
find myself positively *missing* faraway Beatles. "Have
you ever been to Mount Vernon?" I asked. "Such a lovely day, let's drive down." Helen's enthusiasm told me
she was already bored with ruralizing, but she was
sincerely enchanted with the house, lingering before
every room and exclaiming over furnishings.

"I had no idea it was so lovely, Binks," she said,
walking back to the car. "Thanks so much for bringing
me." For half the way home, she talked animatedly of
the china, the fabrics, the wine cooler. Then she sat
silent for a mile or two. "I'm sorry I was a cat last
night, Bi," she said suddenly. I'll back you about the
money, of course; just tell me what to say, and never
mind Rafe."

"I don't need anything but the truth, and I'm positive Rafe needn't know," I said warmly. "Thanks,
sweetie."

"You're welcome," she returned politely, and spoilt it
with a giggle. "What's a bit of perjury between friends,
if needed?"

On Wednesday we went to the National Gallery and
took turns pushing each other in a rolling chair,
whereby our feet were only half as tired as they might
have been. They were still weary enough to make early
bed attractive. Beneath her praise of dinner and in-
consequential chat, I sensed Helen was nervous.
Still worrying about Rafe . . .

She wandered back and forth from dining room to
kitchen, while I put away food and left pots and
plates ready for Peace Beloved in the morning, and in
the living room she looked at me apologetically over

her coffee. "I'm restless, sweetie—how about a game
of gin?"

I got the cards, and said on impulse, "What stakes?
Sky's the limit!"

Her eyes flew upward to meet mine. "Dollar a
point, five a frame, and triple for Schneider," she said
mechanically, shuffling the cards, "but—you *never*
gamble, Binks!"

"Mrs. Ludovic Trael didn't gamble," I shrugged,
lightly, reaching over to cut for deal and turning up
the two of clubs. "Yours, sweetie . . . Let me get another pack of cigarettes."

An hour later, Helen owed me approximately three
thousand dollars and I was feeling slightly sick, between her strained ashen face and my mind saying,
Lucky in love and vice versa . . . I threw in the cards
and said, "Forgive, sweetie? I'm too tired to add up . . ."

"I can't keep my eyes open," she agreed instantly.
"I'll have to give you a check for this, Bi."

"In the morning, when we can see straight," I
pushed away from the table. "I'm for a book and bed,
how about you?"

"A fantabulous suggestion!" She stood up, smoth-
ering a yawn and peered at the bookshelves. "Something easy on eyes and brain—a McGuffey's Reader
would be perfect!"

"Tourism *is* tiresome," I grinned, and sent her off
with a detective story I'd found amusing. Sleepily,
I locked up the house, turned off lights and scanned
the gin rummy score—before shredding and depositing
it in the trash. If Helen could lose three thousand in
an hour to me, it was no longer surprising she should
have lost Rafe's furnishing allowance—and equally not
surprising she should fear his learning of it. I went up
to bed, feeling desperately sad and sorry, remembering
the feverish avidity I'd seen in gambling casinos all
over the world.

Ludo must know Helen's illness, but it would be a family silence, of course—and since I didn't gamble aside from a mild flutter if Ludo took me to Le Touquet or Monte Carlo, I'd never known. I *did* know Helen played cards for money, liked a stake of some sort, but when I'd said I *didn't* ever, with people I knew, she had agreed wholeheartedly. "It does sort of bring out a side one never suspected!"

"Yes, and it's something I'd rather not know about my friends," I said, but in any case I was mostly too busy for afternoon bridge parties, so I'd never known until tonight what Helen considered "a stake."

Like me, Ludo enjoyed the *game;* he'd played bridge for a tenth, occasionally, or a dollar a rubber. He always set the stakes, if there were any; sometimes I didn't even know we were playing for money, and unconsciously I'd always assumed Helen played in the same bracket.

There was a line of light around her closed door. "Good night," I called, and heard her answering, "Sleep tight, sweetie!" I managed half a chapter of the book I was working on before my eyes refused to focus. I fumbled for the lamp switch and was instantly asleep—only to be wide awake an hour later, a phenomenon known to every overtired person.

I propped myself up, slid into my bed jacket, and was reaching for a cigarette when I was aware of motion, a faint *clink*. Opening my door, I peered into darkness. Helen's door was half-open, but there was a faint light downstairs. I flipped the light switch and pattered down the stairs. "Helen?"

"Yes," she said from the kitchen. "I didn't mean to wake you, Binks, but I couldn't sleep, after all. I thought, perhaps a glass of milk . . ."

"I couldn't sleep either, we're overtired. *Tomorrow* we stay home!" I poured milk into a pan. "A dash of brandy and nutmeg?"

She nodded, perching silently on a stool and fumbling in the pocket of her robe for a cigarette, "You destroyed the score, didn't you?" she remarked after a while. "Why, Binks?"

So that was what had kept her awake, drawn her downstairs to stand shivering over the record of her sickness, wondering how to pay. "Of course," I said with a show of surprise. "Weren't we just funning?"

"Were we? Didn't you expect to pay *me* if I'd won?"

"If you wanted, but why would you? All in the family, after all."

"But you *aren't* family now, are you, Bi? You can't play Lady Bountiful any longer, knowing there's more where that came from," she said in an undertone, and smiled faintly at my startled face. "You haven't had to think of money for years; it's a hard habit to break."

"True," I agreed, pouring warm milk into cups, "but I never lived at your pace—and I'm far from broke by my standards." Extending the cup, I caught a flicker in her eyes that I couldn't interpret.

"So you were smart enough to get a settlement," she remarked, accepting the cup. "I wish I had, but it never occurred to me—until I found Rafe hadn't a feather to fly with." She stood up, turning to the hall. "Back to bed!" She was just closing her door as I reached the upper hall. "Good night, again," she smiled gaily. "Sorry I woke you, Bi."

I crawled into bed and sipped the milk, but somewhere a couple of wheels were churning—sluggishly, but picking up speed.

Why didn't Helen know I was meant to be at Casa de Burlas, Perryn's "Fun House?" First she'd said Perryn was worried about me, relieved when she said she'd stay with me—then she'd said *Rafe* had told her and sanctioned her visit . . . and only a few moments ago she'd said, "But you *aren't* family . . ."

All the fear and distrust returned. I set the cup on the bed table, turned off the lamp and sat, concentrating, in the dark. I remembered David Corey's con-

sternation when I said Mrs. Rafe was with me; he'd
wanted desperately to send us both to New Mexico.
I wondered exactly what Helen *did* know; perhaps I
should have probed a bit. They wouldn't have told
her much—but out of her ignorance, I might have
learned whether or not Perryn had actually left New
York? Instead, she'd impulsively flown to Washington, where she was undoubtedly gumming the works!

They'd thought I'd be out of the way. Why was that
important? Something to do with the diaries, of course
—but I hadn't reacted according to plan. Grimly I
thought I would continue to louse up the deal, whatever it was. Tomorrow I would rise, as always, before
Helen, and I would transfer those books to the bank;
there had to be some sort of vault for things that
wouldn't fit into the usual box—and once I'd got them
into the bank, they'd play hell getting them back until
I had a *full* explanation.

I ground out my cigarette in the ashtray—and was
suddenly aware of solitude. *Where was Arthur?*

I slid into my robe again and went out to the study
annex; occasionally, he took a siesta on the cot, although I had a dismal certainty I hadn't seen him in
hours. There was no response to my whisper, and I
went out through Julian's study to the stairs. Helen's
light was out; I could hear regular breathing when I
paused. I went down to the lower hall, growing more
and more anxious. There were a number of *large* dogs
in the neighborhood, with the sort of owners who
think it's "cute" to say *sickem*. I could recall giving
Arthur his dinner, hours ago—and propping the back
door open while I took the garbage out. He'd slipped
out, of course, and unless I were on the *qui vive*, his
voice was always too gentle to be heard.

I flipped the dining room switch—and faced Arthur,
walking in from the kitchen. "Hello, where were you,
I was worried," I whispered, limp with relief. He said
"Mmmwow," softly, but his voice sounded troubled

and he cocked his head to look back to the cellar stairs.

"Come on, silly. There aren't any mice; you got the only one there ever was," I assured him. With my hand on the switch, I had an impulse to verify . . . I went into the living room, with Arthur padding after me, and turned on the Babbitt-type bridge lamp at the end of the couch. Going over to the bookshelves, I leaned to peer beyond the pile of magazines.

Behind me Arthur uttered a protesting wail of pain, and as I started to turn, something landed with cruel force on the back of my head, pitching me forward and downward into the heavy chair blocking the lower shelves. . . .

Chapter
10

The room was in darkness, Arthur was anxiously licking my face, and that dratted clock was pealing four. My head pealed a hundred and four when I tried to move, so I stopped moving, and tried to remember where I was. Obviously, not in bed. Apparently on a floor, with something looming over me. I put out a tentative hand and identified the end of the piano. Arthur purred encouragingly and curled up next to me, while I closed my eyes against the pain. If Arthur had been able to bring me a pillow and a blanket, I would probably have slept until daylight, but as it was, I awoke with not only a dull ache in my head, but a crick in my back as well.

At least I was capable of thought. I didn't even turn on a light when I'd pulled myself from under the piano. The chair was askew; I merely stretched a hand down to the bookshelf, knowing I'd encounter empty space. Of course. The diaries were gone. Naturally.

I felt my way to the couch, found a cigarette and was suddenly madder than a Wall Street bull sold short by a bar. All the spunk of that Robinson who was rumored to have sailed with Sir John Hawkyns and been hanged by Spaniards when he failed to get back to his ship after an early Commando raid (due to a sloe-eyed tavern wench) boiled up within me—in direct proportion to the throb in my head. Wincing, I fingered the spot gently, felt a gummy mat of hair that could only be blood. I finished the cigarette, deliberately making myself limp and nerveless, to build a little strength. Finally I went to the medicine cabinet in the loo for aspirin . . . and drawing a glass of water at the sink, I was aware of lights in the house next door.

At four in the morning?

I swallowed four aspirin, leaning against the counter, and nearly everything fell into place with an almost audible *click.*

Papa—who did puzzles for the Government and cryptograms for fun . . . George, who was a photographer and a bum, who'd photographed Helen and inadvertently learned about the Traels . . . Helen, who was a gambler and afraid of her husband . . . and, finally, Arthur—*who'd been locked out,* but had waited patiently by the back door until someone had snicked the latch, and someone else had stolen in after we were presumably asleep.

But Arthur had slipped in, too—a small black shadow, unnoticed until I had turned on the dining room light—when the intruder had retreated into the dark of the cellar steps. Arthur had known he was there; he'd been troubled, peering anxiously over his shoulder—and I had thought only of mice.

Helen had slipped the latch—on instructions from Perryn? She'd given herself away when she said, "But you *aren't* family, Bi." I'd been too stupid to evaluate that, properly. I'd thought only that Helen didn't know Perryn meant to find Ludo and clear things up . . . now I realized she knew perfectly well it was never intended to clear *anything.*

Never mind the why or wherefore. Action was required. Fleetingly I wondered why Perryn hadn't simply taken the diaries with him—but of course it was more involving for *me* if he left them . . . and glancing in the bookshelves for something to read, Helen had easily found them. *So much for the Pur-*

loined Letter, why in hell hadn't I taken the things
down to lock in Polly's cabinet?

Because I was a gullible ninny and a bumbler! I
should have had those things out of the house, no
matter what! I should have called the FBI myself—
put them in the trunk of the Volkswagen, or thrown
them in the trash can—or torn them up and flushed
them down the loo, I thought furiously—and the hell
with everyone!

Looking at the basement lights next door, I knew
the plan: George was photographing the books—to
be returned through the kitchen door (which was
still unlatched). They meant then to relock the door;
papa Crosson would transcribe at leisure, and for
every future information leak, *I* would be blamed—
but Arthur, bless him, had put a spanner in the works!

He *was* a very good cat!

Had they thought I'd be unconscious until the job
was finished? Certainly they hadn't been *happy* to find
me awake and hunting for my cat. *That* wasn't part
of the plan! It might be inconclusive, but if I went to
the FBI tomorrow with this bruise—and if I locked
the door so they *couldn't* replace the diaries?

I debated. I was definitely going to do something;
what would be the most irritating, most unexpected
action—what would George . . . and Ludo and Perryn . . . never anticipate?

*That I would revive and retrieve the books, of
course.*

I crawled up the stairs, avoiding squeaks as best I
could, but Helen seemed undisturbed. Silently, I
found dark slacks, tennis shoes, black T-shirt; silently
I moved downstairs, one step at a time on my rump,
to avoid creaks. Arthur came with me, obviously at a
loss to understand the peregrinations. At the kitchen
door, I whispered, "You stay here—and if I don't come
back, phone the police!"

"Mmmmwow," he murmured reassuringly—and I slid out the door, half-thinking he'd do it, too.

There was a light in papa's study as well as the basement. It was a dark night, but they might notice motion; I got down on my tummy and slithered over the grass to the rear of the garage, where I picked up a sturdy billet of firewood, on impulse. If someone had knocked me on the head, I might as well be prepared to return the compliment.

It was an unexpectedly warm night, and I was perspiring in the T-shirt—but the heat proved helpful: George had left the rear door ajar for air. Crawling forward in the shadows, I saw I was right: very carefully, he was taking photographs of each page of a diary, held in a wire frame and lit by two huge floodlights that he repositioned occasionally. The rest of the notebooks were piled on a table just inside the door, and unconsciously I counted them: eight . . . plus the one in the frame—and there had been ten, so papa must be transcribing one directly, up in the study.

Or perhaps Ludo was reading it for him?

Or Perryn? I'd only his word Ludo'd never taught him the code . . .

George suddenly switched off the floodlights and took a roll of film away to the bedroom. *Starting to develop at once,* I thought, and wished I knew more about photography. He'd half closed the bedroom door to the rec room; how long before he'd return? I was already slipping down the back steps, reaching in and scooping the pile of diaries on the table into my arms . . . retreating into the shadows toward the garage. While I slid the things between the pile of firewood and the garage wall, I was entirely calm and fearless, wondering with academic detachment whether there'd be time to retrieve the one he was working on?

Briefly, I debated. I'd got all but two; discretion is

always the better part of valor. Why not return to Julian's house, lock the door behind me and phone both local police and FBI?

"Because as soon as George finishes this one, he will look for the others—which will instantly reveal jiggery-pokery—and long before the Law arrives he will have flitted with what they already have . . . leaving papa to explain that Miss Robinson is simply a hysterical woman."

Could I make a case for myself, lacking those two diaries? Perhaps, but meanwhile George and papa Crosson would be getting away with something—and I had been bopped on the head and was just plain *mad* . . . to say nothing of those filthy pictures, undoubtedly produced with the floodlights and darkroom before me.

George reappeared. He didn't notice the disappearance of the pile of diaries, but returned to neatly filming the one on the frame. It seemed an age before he removed another roll of film and went off to the darkroom. The instant he'd vanished, I flew across and wrenched the diary from its holder—but this time luck was against me; he'd only gone for a fresh roll of film.

As I turned, he was standing in the bedroom doorway, and there was a most unpleasant little gun in his hand. "Well, well," he drawled, in the sort of oily seductive voice that says *I am irresistible to women, poor things.* He came toward me with a self-satisfied smile (and a wave of cheap gin), saying easily, "What have we here?"

"Unexpected company," I told him sweetly—and brought my billet of firewood crashing full force across his wrist. The gun went off, of course, somewhere into the floor, and he dropped it with a howl and lunged for me. "Bitch!" he snarled.

So I bopped *him* on the head.

He went down with a crash, and I wondered with

detachment whether I'd killed him, while upstairs a voice called, "George?" I was so flown with success at that point that I held my hand over my mouth, deepened my voice as much as possible, and growled "Darkroom." George had a nasty tenor voice, and for a woman, mine is very brunette—so apparently it satisfied papa at a range of two floors.

I looked at George, huddled on the floor, and I suppose I went berserk. First, I went into the darkroom and dragged all the soaking film out to the floodlights. Then I pulled all his supply of unused film into the deepest trough, and daintily emptied every bottle, every pan, over it. I folded all the portable smashable glass in the blanket and quilt on his bed, and belted it with the firewood. It cracked sharply, but not loudly enough to disturb papa, two floors up. There was a small file built under the developing pans. It was filled with neatly labeled folders of negatives. There was nothing under Trael, or Robinson, or "Fakes"—I couldn't think of any other suitable classification, but perhaps he kept such things under his pillow at night?

Coldly, I transferred all the envelopes of negatives to the sitz-bath-shower and set a match to them. It was the most *beautiful* mess by the time I got through . . .

Every once in a while I checked on George, who was breathing but still out. I considered giving him another *bop* but decided against. It might prove one too many, since I am a bumbler who is not trained in the science of bopping. *Leave him lay*, I decided—because the one thing I wanted was for George to revive to chaos, and serve him bloody well right. That would teach him not to fake filthy pictures of women he didn't even know!

There was still a bit to do. I poked the diary he'd been filming behind a small shrub beside the cellar steps. I set camera and tripod plus floodlights quietly on the floor; George's gun was still there, so I picked it up and stuck it in my slacks pocket, hoping to heaven the thing wasn't poised to go off and shoot me in the leg—because I was definitely going to *try* to get upstairs for the last diary.

George groaned slightly, but his eyes were still closed. With *infinite* joy and great care, I poised the firewood billet—and smashed downward with every bit of my strength: first the camera lens, then the floodlights. There was a series of splintering bangs and crashes not to be overlooked by papa Crosson, and even as I fled up to the kitchen and into the shadows of the living room, I could hear alarmed motion above.

A door opened onto the upper hall, and to my horror, I could hear not one—but *two* voices. *"George?"*

Well, I'm not cut out for anything more than brushing my teeth every morning. *I* had never thought of possible reinforcement. I'd thought papa would trot *down* to investigate the noise; I would trot *up* to snatch the final notebook and, optimistically, I'd thought I'd be able to get back to the lower hall while he was assessing the damage in the basement and reviving George. The open back door might be a useful red herring, to delay him briefly . . . and meanwhile I'd be out the *front* door, into the shadows of the porch and hedge. Crouching at the end of the sofa, I could dimly see that the front door had only the usual burglar lock—no chain or slide bolts.

I could hear consultation in the upper hall; perhaps they'd both go down to check? But after two more importunate calls for "George? What's wrong?" my blood froze—as the second voice emerged from the study and was clear to my ears.

"George! Damn the fellow, he's drunk again; I told you not to let him have that last highball. Once he gets going, he won't stop . . . he got the flask from the car, boozing downstairs—he'll ruin everything. I'll check, while you go on, Sandor . . ." The voice approached,

with footsteps coming quickly down the stairs to the hall.

And the voice was that of Ralph Trael.

I couldn't believe it—yet I couldn't be mistaken after four years . . . and peeking around the edge of the sofa, I could identify Rafe—in slacks and impeccable silk sport shirt, pivoting himself on the newel post, headed for kitchen and basement.

So all the Traels were in this together?

Now my heart was really pumping with fear. I must, *I must*, get out of this house . . . but Sandor Crosson was lingering at the top of the stairs. Momentarily Rafe would discover the shambles in the cellar. I held my breath and *willed* Crosson to go back to the study and eventually he retreated, judging by the sounds. I sprinted for the door, fumbling desperately for the locks, and just as I'd turned them—was nearly out and away to safety—Rafe yelled urgently, *"Sandor!"*

It seemed every light in the place went on instantly—and I was spotlighted against the hall door, with a slender black-clad male figure descending the stairs. He was holding a gun, and he saw me at once. I could hear Rafe coming up from the cellar, while Sandor Crosson and I regarded each other silently. "Dear me, what an *inconvenient* young woman you are, Miss Robinson," he murmured regretfully, holding the gun very steady.

I was quite aware he'd have no hesitation in using it. I looked at him thoughtfully. "You know—I consider that comment . . . considering its source . . . among the highest accolades I shall ever receive," I told him judicially . . . just as Rafe came into the hall from the kitchen—and stopped dead at sight of me.

"You!" he said, and went dead white.

I'd always thought Rafe was Cardinal Richelieu in modern dress. Fleetingly now, I wondered why I'd never thought until this moment that Richelieu was also not anyone's concept of a sweet little household pet . . .

"We have flushed a very pretty pigeon, as you see, Rafe," Crosson was saying, leaning over the stair rail. "What shall we do with her, I wonder?"

Rafe ignored him. He walked forward slowly, producing a gun of his own. "You interfering bitch," he said softly. "I've had four years of your sweetness and light — ruining everything in my life. I won't take any more of it. Once and for all, I'll get rid of you . . ."

From the stairs, Crosson said sharply, "No—*not here!* Cover her, while I get Roden; let him deal with her."

Nervously, my fingers were plucking at the knob behind my back. I could feel it moving, opening— but could I widen the crack until I could whirl outside and run—run—*run?* Rafe would shoot instantly if I moved, but perhaps a bullet wouldn't penetrate the door?

He was walking forward slowly, his dark eyes glittering feverishly. "He's insane," I thought, and knew it was literally true. For some reason, Rafe hated me, wanted to kill me. *He was my enemy*—why hadn't I known it?

"You ruined everything," he said again, and the calm conversational tone was more frightening than violence. "Because of you, I would never have my inheritance. All the years of planning—*wasted*. You took him away, *you* had to be first. *You* pushed me into the cold, you'd stop at nothing," he chuckled sardonically, "but you got fooled: you *couldn't* have children, after all." Rafe laughed softly. "Well, at least we're equals there—even if for different reasons."

Crosson was now thoroughly alarmed, and inching down the stairs unobtrusively, muttering, "Hold it, Rafe! For God's sake . . ." but Rafe was beyond reason, and I knew it.

So I was going to die. Very well. My fingers released the doorknob behind me and I positioned myself for easy shooting. "Go ahead, Rafe," I said, with insulting indifference, "but you'll never find the rest of Ludo's diaries. *He'll* be safe, at least."

Crosson was obviously going to *try* to prevent Rafe. *Spots on the carpet,* I thought frivolously, *blood is very hard to remove, mama won't like it!* "Rafe *listen!*" he was babbling, urgently, "let me get Roden—we can handle it, don't worry—but *not here!*"

"I'll handle it myself," Rafe said, "and don't try to stop me Sandor. This is a moment I shall enjoy . . ."

"Drop the gun, brother," Ludo's deep voice said quietly from the kitchen doorway—and everything happened at once.

The door behind me was violently thrust open, knocking me forward to the floor, and two men with guns said, "Drop 'em!" It was too late to halt Rafe's automatic reflex; one of the men got the bullet meant for me in his shoulder. The other man unerringly got a bullet to Rafe's gun arm. Crosson said, "Don't shoot!" and dropped his gun, raising his arms quickly.

Perryn stood in the archway to the living room. He had a gun, too. It was pointed at Rafe.

I rolled aside and up to my knees, pressing a hand to my mouth and aware I was whimpering hysterically, while the unwounded man quietly picked up Crosson's gun and nudged him down the stairs and out to the porch in silence. Vaguely, I realized there were other figures, in the shadows behind Ludo and Perryn, moving about on the driveway and porch. No one said anything.

Rafe stood, cornered between his brothers, the gun arm hanging limp, with blood welling slowly into a vicious stain disfiguring the Honan silk of his shirt. He looked at Perryn. "Two against one," he said impersonally. "That's the way it always was, wasn't it?"

With astonishing swiftness, he whirled on Ludo. "All right, I'm a DeCourcy—*not* a Trael," he said deliberately. "We always knew that, didn't we? Look after Nell—*brother* . . ."

His left hand dragged the wounded gun arm upward, and involuntarily I screamed. For the second time in my life I fainted as the gun went off—but this time I revived in Heaven.

I was lying across Ludo's lap, my head against his shoulder and his voice saying frantically, "Where's the doctor? Bi, beloved—speak to me!"

And as previously, my mind was extraordinarily clear. "What would you like me to say?" I asked.

It was astonishingly simple. "Do you—*love* me?" Ludo asked, impersonally.

I looked squarely into the clear blue eyes and remembered Perryn's "explanation" of Ludo. "Yes," I said. "I loved you at least as soon as you loved me—and possibly a few seconds earlier and as soon as I get over this hit on the head, I will enumerate all the *ways* in which I love you, and the whys and wherefores—but at the moment, I'm *tired*."

"*Hit in the head?*" he echoed. "*Who* hit you? *When*, why, where . . . Good God, *where* is the doctor?" he said in his lion roar . . . and somebody came over to do something painful to the sore spot on my head. Somebody else said urgently, "Where *are* the diaries, Mrs. Trael?" and still wincing from the antiseptic, I said, "I am *not* Mrs. Trael, I am Miss Robinson—and the diaries are behind my woodpile, next to the garage, ooooh!"

Ludo said deeply, "My *wife* is exhausted, no more questions now. I'll take her home," and simply *stood up*, holding me as casually as a baby.

The first fingers of dawn were shooting into the sky behind the magnificent Cedar of Lebanon across the street; there were a dozen cars parked here and there, and Julian's house was ablaze with light. There were lights in other houses, too, and my heart sank, remembering Julian's plea, "Polly and I have to come back there!" Just as Ludo carried me down the steps and out to the sidewalk, a sort of covered basket was inserted into a wagon, which quietly drove away. Two male figures were being shepherded into another car.

"Where's Suzanne?" I asked anxiously. "Ludo—she mustn't know!"

"Shhh, she and her mother are still asleep," he said reassuringly. "They'd both been given mild sedatives, so they wouldn't hear anything, I suppose. Don't try to talk, dearest."

"Helen?" I whispered, while he was tucking me into bed.

"She's quite all right. Go to sleep, beloved," Ludo said gently. "Tomorrow will be time enough."

He'd made someone bring up the biggest wing chair and the ottoman. When I woke, he was still loosely holding my hand, but fast asleep, with his feet propped uncomfortably. His face was gaunt and disastrously thin, defenseless in sleep, and there were three white hairs in the russet over one temple.

I lay very quietly, looking at My Man and feeling a bit medieval—because how many husbands will rescue a wife from peril these days? The bedside clock said eleven-thirty, and Arthur was insinuating himself through the crack to the study annex. He leapt onto the bed and made his way to lick my nose anxiously. "Mmmmwow?"

"Shhh," I whispered reassuringly, "I'm all right. Thanks for sending the police, but don't talk; daddy's asleep."

"No, he isn't," Ludo said, his eyes still closed. "What am I fathering?"

"Arthur."

Arthur stepped across me on delicate paws, sniffed Ludo's fingers briefly. "*Mmmmmwow!*" he said definitively, and established himself on Ludo's knees at once, going round and round to be comfortable and blinking at me apologetically when finally settled.

I got the message. "I'm with you," I assured him, while Ludo opened his eyes lazily, to assess Arthur, raise a hand to tickle beneath the throat, and look at me with a sudden convulsive clench of the hand holding mine.

"Really *you*," he sighed incredulously.

"I've cut my hair," I said. I always believe in getting over heavy ground as lightly as possible.

"I wouldn't care if you were bald, so long as it's you."

"Enough of this lovemaking!" Perryn said in a bogus Russian accent. "The place is crawling with people, and Peace Beloved is popping her gum every two seconds." He came forward from the study annex lazily and leaned on the back of Ludo's chair, looking down at Arthur. "Sycophant," he said severely. "Toadeater!"

"Mmmwow," Arthur said apologetically, and crawled up Ludo's chest, to place a paw on either shoulder and lick his nose.

"Get a cat of your own, brother," Ludo advised, blandly, transferring Arthur to the floor and standing up. His head was about two inches below the ceiling and when Perryn stood up, his head was nearly as high. The room, in fact, was cluttered with Traels. "Go away, so I can *breathe?*"

It was a full hour before I could pull myself together, dress and go down the stairs. There were too many reminders—such as the master bedroom, bare of Helen's monogrammed luggage, with beds already neatly made and covered with Polly's sham-candlewick bedspreads—and the first blossom on the bush Suzanne and I had been nursing along toward the Rose Show . . . I sat for a long while, one stocking on and one off, facing the fact that Rafe was dead . . . and Helen was a widow . . .

Because of me . . .

Last night Ludo'd chosen his wife at the expense of his brother. For the rest of his life, I thought sadly, he would never really be able to forget that—and I would forever have to be worth such a choice. Of course, I wasn't, I never could be . . .

I came downstairs to find Peace Beloved in charge. "You has your breakfast *first*, Miss Robinson," she stated, and when Ludo and Perryn started to accompany me to the dining room, she turned on them coldly. "We eats *alone*," she said firmly. "We don't want no burps from nervous indigestion. You-all go talk to your friends until Miss Robinson is ready to receive you."

Ludo drew himself up and said in a modified lion roar, "Miss Robinson is *my wife*," but Peace Beloved was not quelled. She stepped back one pace and eyed him up and down.

"So you says," she observed disdainfully, "but if she your wife, *where was you?*" She turned her back with finality and ushered me tenderly to the dining table, while Perryn remarked irrepressibly, "A good question, brother. Shall we join the throng?"

Ludo's face went dark with anger, until I said quietly, "It *is* a good question, Ludo—but I'd like it answered later, please."

He stood, hesitant and reluctant, with Perryn pulling him away; it was touch and go whether he'd submit to command . . . but Peace Beloved trotted in with the coffee pot and a fluffy omelette flanked by sausage cakes. She set them before me, cast a glance of the most consummate indifference at Ludo's towering figure and observed, "*You* still here? Didn't I already *tell* you to go away? Mr. Perryn—get rid of him!"

I looked at Ludo with a smile. "If you go away

now," I murmured, "it will allow time for Peace Beloved to prepare a really satisfying brunch for you later . . ."

"All right," he said, after a moment, "but you realize, I'm—afraid to let you out of my sight?"

The questions were endless, although the men from the FBI and the State Department were enormously polite and considerate, almost flattering. Once I was fed, Peace Beloved had relented, and she was whisking in with plates of hot cakes, sausages, bacon, hot toast, portions of corned beef hash gussied up with onion and grated cheese. When she appeared with plates of crisp tacos and Mrs. Somebody's Clam Sticks, I realized we were scraping the bottom of the barrel . . . but with Ludo's strong arm around me, who cared?

Sid Abelson and Mr. Anscot arrived—in separate taxis—about two o'clock. Ludo stood up casually. "*I* sent for you, so we can finish this thing today. Perryn —ask Peace Beloved for more food and coffee; she doesn't approve of me yet."

I sat on the couch and answered questions. "No, I never met George Lavretta; I never saw Mr. Crosson, never knew where he worked. His daughter only said they didn't like questions because of his job—I thought perhaps he was a T-man."

"He worked in the coding department for European affairs for the State Department, Mrs. Trael," Lawson, the senior FBI agent, told me.

I nodded. "That figures. Suzanne told me her father did puzzles for fun at home, and they were obviously cryptograms—but I thought he might be in any of the scientific groups."

"You never asked?"

"Heavens, no—I wasn't interested . . . and anyway . . ." I told them about snoopy Miss King, which drew involuntary chuckles.

"Did you ever at any time transcribe any part of Mr. Trael's diaries for anyone, Mrs. Trael?" Lawson asked finally.

I shook my head. "Not really. I picked out all the place names for Mr. Perryn Trael—but you *know* that . . . and I'm *not* Mrs. Trael."

There was a minute silence, before Sid Abelson and Mr. Anscot simultaneously cleared their throats with neat attorney "erhmmmmm!" There was then a silent visual consultation along the lines of "After you, my dear Alphonse,"—following which, Sid said, "But the divorce is not yet final, Bianca—there's another three weeks to go . . ."

"And," said Mr. Anscot meticulously, "if Mr. Ludovic Trael should fail to pick up the papers, I fear you would still be legally his wife. Oh, dear!" he said under his breath—so like the White Rabbit that involuntarily I murmured, "Oh, my dear paws and whiskers . . ."

We finally got rid of everybody, including Anscot and Sid Abelson, who grinned at me fleetingly where I was lying on the couch (because Ludo said I was exhausted and enough was enough). "When you have the story, let me hear it, Bianca? Or as much as you can tell—because there's obviously a happy ending."

Finally, there was only Ludo and myself—with Perryn tactfully joshing Peace Beloved in the kitchen . . . and no food in the house, and a key inserted in the front door lock.

Perryn emerged like a coiled watchspring from the kitchen, and Ludo stood up, moving back to the end of the couch, with a gun suddenly poised in his hand. The door swung open finally, a travelling bag *clunked* on the hall floor, a warm feminine voice called, "Bi? Where are you? Aunt Bianca?"

"I'm here." I rolled around Ludo's bulk and ran forward, to hug Phebe gently. "Why are you here?"

"Daddy was worried; you didn't write last Sunday," she stripped off her gloves efficiently and eyed Ludo's towering figure. "Does this ichthyosaurus belong to you? I thought you were on your own."

"That's Ludo . . ."

"And I am *not* an ichthyosaurus!"

Phebe looked at him again, indifferently. "No," she agreed. "Too short a neck. Bi, if you're all right, catch that cab—I might as well go back again . . ."

"My brother is a tyrannosauraus," said Perryn, reproachfully. He was leaning, casually, arms folded, against the jamb of the dining room archway, and from the glint in his eyes surveying Phebe's slender height and natural ash-blonde hair . . .

She swung about to stare at him. "Perryn, this is my niece: Phebe," I said casually, hearing the taxi revving outside and zooming away.

Phebe's eyes are the color of ripe damson plums, which is pretty astounding beneath natural ash-blonde hair. Perryn took one look and straightened up. "Can you cook?" he inquired.

"Yes—but I'm better with complex computers," Phebe told him calmly. "What do you do?"

"I manage a cattle ranch."

"Well," said Phebe after a moment, her eyes still locked with Perryn's. "I *suppose* we could compute how many calves are likely . . . or something?"

"And I suppose you could go to market," I said, pathetically. "D'you mind, Phibs? Perryn will drive you over . . . I'm a little tired."

"No," she said absently, still looking at Perryn. "What shall I get?"

"Whatever you like," I said gently, "including Green Stamps."

"I'm sorry about Rafe," I whispered a while later. "You know that?"

"Yes."

"I don't have to have answers now—but someday, please?"

"Yes." Ludo stood up, dwarfing the room and looking down at me. "There will never, to all eternity, be any way to erase this," he said sadly. "I might as well have shot myself—like Rafe."

"Oh *no!*"

He turned away briefly, found cigarettes and lighter—set an ashtray within reach—and sat down crosslegged on the floor beside me. "How can I explain it to you?" he murmured, reaching for my hand. "*How will I ever explain it to myself!*" He laid his cheek against my palm, and I said what was the vital question to me.

"Ludo—is it *over?*" When his eyes met mine questioningly, "I mean . . . do you still want me for your wife?" I whispered.

"Yes," he said instantly. "I've never loved, never wanted, any other woman but you, Binks . . . and how *could* I have doubted you!" He closed his eyes and softly kissed my hand. "You'll never be able to forget that I didn't trust you as you trusted me," Ludo said analytically. "You damn near got yourself killed tonight, trying to protect me, and I . . ." he winced and bent his head, "but the divorce," he said strongly, "I knew nothing about it, Bi. I never knew they meant to *use* those pictures, or put Esther and the others on the stand. I swear it!"

"Shhh, it's all right. Forget it."

"I can't—and neither can you," Ludo said flatly, sitting back and lighting a cigarette for both of us. "This is it, Bi; if I hadn't been *stupid*, I'd have known the answer at once.

"Rafe was a DeCourcy—*and the DeCourcys were traitors*," Ludo said quietly. "D'you understand, Bi? The original DeCourcys were deported for political crimes. We all thought it was rather fun—like having a horse thief or a pirate in the family tree . . . but Rafe took it seriously. He looked like the DeCourcys, he identified himself with them when the going got tough.

"He married an expensive free-loader with more Society than Sense, and they really loved each other," Ludo went on, evenly. "But Rafe couldn't give her children, Bi; *he was sterile.* Probably everything would have been different if he'd produced the first son for the family. It wasn't too unbearable so long as I didn't marry . . . and by the time I met you, darling, I'd been around so long, no one ever expected I was going to marry.

"But then I met you—and my reaction was very much like Perryn's half an hour ago," Ludo grinned at me drily. "Within ten days and with no warning whatsoever, I was not only married but to a *young* wife who might produce children to carry on the name . . . and to Rafe, it was *my* children who were important, because of the trust.

"Partly my fault," Ludo said soberly. "I could—I can—dissolve the trust—but I'd never in the world have done it . . . because Rafe would have lost every penny! He had no head for business, Bi; David Corey supervised everything Rafe did . . . but d'you see, Rafe *thought* I was going to dissolve because I wasn't married, didn't have children. When I married you, and when I was evasive about dissolving . . . Rafe thought it was because I hoped for sons of my own.

"That's point one," Ludo said. "Point two is that Helen didn't know until after she was married that Rafe was sterile—and she's a woman who should have had children on whom to concentrate. Instead, she became a gambler, while Rafe was trying to make a coup in the stock market—and most of the time they both lost. Not too bad so long as they lived in my house, because I was paying the bills—but when you chivvied them out of that, Rafe couldn't cope.

"Helen had gotten into the big time gambling, through George Lavretta." Ludo's face went grim.

"The pictures . . ."

Ludo was silent for a minute. "There were two things," he said, finally. "Lavretta boasted about his brother-in-law in the State Department who could break *any* code. Helen hadn't the faintest idea of what was in those notebooks, Binks—but at some point she gave one, at random, to Lavretta. It was more or less 'Your brother-in-law is so smart? Let's see what he makes of this'!"

"And Crosson deciphered it quite easily. It was never meant to be anything but a time-saver, Binks," Ludo said. "Of course, being in the State Department, he saw the possibilities of the information. He insisted George should get any more information available . . . and meanwhile Rafe had stumbled on those negatives of you. I'd had them in my desk, *meaning* to discard them, so I wasn't surprised they were gone.

"And simultaneously Rafe had tumbled to Helen's flirtation with Lavretta." Ludo stood up suddenly and paced the room, his back to me. "Rafe knew—my temper, my jealousy," he said in a low voice. "He had Lavretta make up the pictures, saying they were only for a practical joke . . . and when the psychological moment arose, Rafe sent them to me."

He turned to look at me. "You will never forget them, Bi," he said impersonally, "or that I took them seriously. Perryn told me . . . and it's true I didn't, couldn't, look at them closely—but I should have *believed* you, and I didn't, while you really never stopped believing in me."

"Well, I wouldn't say that," I murmured. "I thought you'd had the pictures made in order to marry someone else—and I was making a wax figure, in my spare time. She was going to have the most *terrible* headaches."

Ludo smiled at me absently, but his eyes were still

intent. "Well—George put the finger on Helen to get the rest of my notebooks—and Helen owed him so much money, she couldn't well refuse, but she was still so uneasy that she finally told Rafe. She put it on the basis of: she'd only been calling Lavretta's bluff —and now that he wanted some more, what should she do?

"Rafe said he'd handle it," Ludo went on slowly. "Apparently, he made a deal with Lavretta for a cut of any profits . . . but Helen didn't know that for some time." He looked down at me impersonally. "You loved Helen, didn't you?"

"Next to you . . ."

He nodded. "Then you'll understand, because I think she loved you next to Rafe—and it really was difficult for her to involve you . . . but Rafe told her to get the rest of the diaries. So Helen went over to the house, the day you were packing," his face twisted, agonized, "and just as she had the notebooks in her hands, she heard someone coming . . . so she jettisoned them into the nearest valise, and went away, waiting for a chance to get them back.

"Next thing she knew, everything was sealed and being carried out of the place. She had no idea where you were, but of course she assumed the diaries were in a valise being taken to your hotel . . . and apparently, the packers rearranged the books into the carton. When you phoned her, Rafe was there. He came with her, of course; she was to visit you while he searched for the notebooks—but instead, they found you asleep . . . and no sign of the books. Next day, you were gone.

"Rather a good joke for you to turn up in the house next to Crosson!" Ludo remarked. "He'd never seen you, and once you'd cut your hair, even George didn't recognize you quickly. Perryn put most of it together when he found you, although he thought it was just Helen, but he never told either of them where you

were. Helen twigged it when Esther said Perryn had
called her from your brother's house."

"I thought Perryn had sent her to go to the ranch
with me, for company."

Ludo nodded soberly. "By that time, the FBI were
fairly sure I'd been right in the beginning, after all—
although they hadn't any clue to Crosson, until Perryn
got hold of them in New York. They *didn't* know
where I was, and they were putting pressure on Interpol when Perryn arrived . . ."

"Where were you, anyway—or can't you tell?" I
asked, idly, admiring his broad shoulders and straight
spine, as always.

Ludo looked at me silently for a moment, then his
lips twitched. "I was exactly where you said I'd be,"
he remarked, gently, "and the instant Perryn told the
FBI, Interpol found me *and* the Ariel within two
hours . . . and the instant they got me, I took the next
plane."

"So Perryn never went to Lisbon after all?"

Ludo shook his head. "Wasn't necessary; I was on
the way back, so he simply waited for me in New
York, thinking all the time that you were safe in New
Mexico—until Drummond phoned you'd never arrived, and David found you were still here, *with
Helen!* Perryn was so certain she was behind the
whole thing, he was scared to death, but the FBI
persuaded him they'd protect you." He snorted slightly and knelt down beside me. "And a lousy job they
did, you still got hit on the head!"

"Well, they couldn't know I'd be looking for Arthur at the wrong moment," I pointed out. "Did they
see George coming to get the diaries?"

"Oh yes," he nodded, "and they did think he was
pretty sure of himself to be turning on lights, but
naturally they thought you were sound asleep upstairs
. . . and they were concentrating on the house next
door, just waiting until Perryn and I arrived. They'd

seen Rafe go in, and they'd traced the connection between Lavretta and Helen, as well as Crosson's job
with the State Department, so they were pretty sure
of the story." He smiled grimly. "They're a bit—embarrassed at the way you got past them to upset the
applecart," he remarked, and put his arms around me
convulsively.

"Oh, Bi—I was such a stupid fool," he groaned,
burying his face against my shoulder.

"Hush, it doesn't matter now."

"No," he agreed, "except you have to know . . ."
Ludo looked at me steadily. "You see, Rafe was—always like that. Even when we were youngsters, you
couldn't entirely rely on what he said or did, Bi. He
did admire me, he was jealous of my friendships—he
was inclined to make trouble, whenever I paid too
much attention to someone else. Then he married
Helen, and he seemed to have transferred his af-
fections entirely to her. It was all so long ago," Ludo
muttered. "I'd forgotten Rafe's jealousy. I never
dreamed he'd transfer it to you, darling."

"He was always a clever conniver," Ludo shrugged.
"He always knew how to divide people for his own
purposes, and when the time came, he knew exactly
how to unsettle me and divide me from you. It was
Rafe who altered the instructions to the lawyer, and
at the same time explaining to me that the FBI insisted on producing all the evidence.

"I knew nothing about it until I was in court," he
said, "and then it was too late. Will you ever forgive
me?"

"Do you love me?" I countered.

"God, yes!"

"Well then—that's all that matters."

We were sitting in one chair on the porch when
Phebe and Perryn came back. I noticed Phebe was
doing nothing but direct the transfer of shopping bags

to the kitchen, and shortly thereafter they came out to join us. Peace Beloved produced a drink tray with snacks, and Arthur inspected Phebe with approval. There were a few roses to contemplate. I drew a long breath unconsciously; it was all over, at last.

In the gathering dusk and desultory conversation, I was suddenly aware that Perryn's hand was holding Phebe's, to the entire satisfaction of both. He caught my eye and grinned.

"So she isn't a sister," he said gently, "she'll still do nicely—thank you!"

Something peculiar is happening in
Port Arbello.
The children are disappearing,
one by one.

Suffer the Children

A Novel by John Saul

An evil history that occurred one hundred years ago
is repeating itself.

Only one man heard a pretty little girl begin to
scream. He watched her struggle and die, then stilled
his guilty heart by dashing himself to death in the
sea . . .

Now that strange, terrified child has ended her silence
with the scream that began a century ago. Don't miss
this tale of unnatural passion and supernatural terror!

A Dell Book $1.95

Dell Bestsellers